Journey of Joy
By Emma Rylin Ballard
Copyright 2016 Emma Rylin Ballard
BZ Publishing LLC
Lancaster Ohio
Happy Eternally After Book 2

Chapter 1

Dawn Elliot used her badge to open the door to the switchboard office. Julie was sitting at the desk chatting with the second shift operator.

Dawn took off her coat and hung it on the back of her chair. The weather was mild for February but not so mild that she could go without a coat and hat. Dawn set her lunchbox and purse into a drawer and clocked in on the computer. She was bursting to talk to Julie but she needed to do it alone. Her news was too personal. Too gut wrenching.

The second shift girl told her about the new process that had been implemented that morning while Julie pushed the computer on wheels, nicknamed the COW, into the hallway to register a patient.

Dawn waited impatiently for the other switchboard operator to clock out and to grab her things. Then, she waited for Julie to return.

Three ER walk in patients and two squads later Julie finally sat down across from her. Julie's chestnut hair was pulled back in a ponytail but strands of it had fallen loose. Her shift had started four hours before Dawn's and Dawn could only guess it had been a rough one. Some days working in a hospital ER were invigorating but some days were draining. She pulled up the ER tracking board and saw that every room was filled and several more patients were in the waiting room. She could guess what kind of night she was in for. It wasn't a shock considering how her morning had gone.

"You don't look so well. Was the test over Don Quixote harder than you expected?"

"The test went fine. It isn't that." Dawn handed her phone to Julie. She had pulled up her social media account that morning and the picture she found had been haunting her all day.

"Ben got married?" Julie asked. She sounded as surprised as Dawn had been.

"In Vegas," Dawn said.

"He looks so different," Julie said. Dawn had to agree. When she had dated Ben he had been the stereotypical returned missionary look wise. Now, his hair was shaggy and he had grown a goatee. Worst still, he now had gauges in his ears and a spider tattoo visible on his neck. Conspicuously absent was the CTR ring his mother had given him before his mission. During the time they had dated she had never seen him remove it.

"Are you alright?" Julie asked handing Dawn back her phone.

"Just shocked I think," Dawn said. She had been pretty sure she was going to marry Ben. Then, she found out he had been living a double life. When he was not doing service projects with her and teaching Sunday school he was out drinking with friends. She had confronted him about it and he had confessed that he had been struggling with his faith ever since his mission and that he planned to leave the church.

"How did you even see this?" Julie asked.

"I guess we still had a few mutual friends," Dawn said with a shrug. She had thought she had wiped him completely out of her life but when she had seen the picture it was as if her heart had broken all over again.

"Maybe this is a blessing in disguise," Julie said. "Perhaps now that you are sure he is not coming back you can start to really move on."

Dawn cringed.

She had gone on a few dates since Ben had left but only two had led to second dates and none to third. She hadn't felt much like putting herself out there since the break up. First, she had been too heartbroken to move on. Then, she had been too busy. Her father had a heart attack and her family had decided to move to Colorado where her father was born and raised. That had necessitated Dawn initially moving in with Julie at her parents' house and then joining Julie as her roommate after she married Denny Miller.

Between moving, work, and her final year of college there just hadn't felt like much time for dating. Plus, somewhere in the deepest parts of her heart, she had hoped that Ben would come back to his faith and to her. Now, he was married to someone else. It really was over.

"I don't suppose this is the time to share my good news," Julie whispered.

"I could use some good news," Dawn said.

"Denny and I are going to have a baby!" Julie said.

"You're pregnant?" Dawn asked. That would be a miracle. Denny had been told by his doctors that he would not be able to have children without medical intervention.

"Not yet," Julie said with a blush. "We made an appointment to see the fertility specialist and talk about the options we have. Initially, we had planned to wait until Denny finished college but since I am finished with school now I didn't want to wait. We have been praying about it and just really feel like we should start working on our family now. The doctors warned us that it could take quite a bit of time. It could be a rough journey," Julie said. Dawn's heart went out to her friend. Julie and Denny were the best people she had ever met and she wished that life could have been easier for them. Denny had been paralyzed by an IED explosion during his military service. He had learned to be self sufficient with the help of Xander, his service dog, but she had seen him struggle to adjust to life without the use of his legs. Thankfully, with the help of Julie, Denny had found purpose in his life and felt called to serve the deaf community. He worked as a TTY relay operator and was going to school to become an interpreter.

"Hopefully I will have my degree and be ready to move out by then," Dawn said. She had less than six months left until she had earned a bachelor's degree in English. Once that happened she wasn't sure what she planned to do.

She might continue school and train to teach though she wasn't really sure if being an English teacher was something she wanted.

She did not see herself in marketing or journalism which many of her classmates planned to enter. In fact, she wasn't at all sure what her long term career goals were. She had majored in English because she thought it would help her feel closer to her mother who had died years before.

"You don't have to move out. Denny and I don't mind you living with us and the house is large enough. Besides, it might be nice to have an extra pair of hands to help with the baby when Denny is busy," Julie said.

"I feel like I am intruding. You and Denny have never really gotten to live alone together," Dawn said.

"And once the baby comes we never will," Julie said with a laugh.

The walkie talkie beeped and a voice said "new patient in bed ten." Julie sighed and stood up.

She grabbed the COW and headed out to the ER corridor.

Dawn took out the stack of paperwork that needed to be done over the course of the night. Denny and Julie were moving on to the next stage of their lives. She wondered when she would be able to do the same.

Isaiah Toppins rolled over with a groan. His body was exhausted but his mind wouldn't let him sleep. He pulled himself up feeling fatigued at the small effort and walked outside to the balcony of Pete's apartment where he was crashing. It was just another place he was passing through. He wanted to get a place of his own but the commissions he was earning at his new job were scant. At this rate, he would be shuffling between couches the rest of his life.

He leaned over the balcony railing and inhaled. It had been raining until just a few moments ago but the smell still hung in the air.

"What do you want me to do?" He said it again and again in his prayers but on nights like this he wondered if

Heavenly Father was listening to him. He felt lost.

The door behind him opened and Pete came out bare foot and rubbing his eyes.

"You alright?"

"Yeah," Isaiah said. "Just enjoying the night air."

"A letter came today. It said return to sender. It was one you sent to Missouri." Every returned letter felt like a rock in the pit of his stomach though he knew they were the most likely outcome.

"Thanks," Isaiah said.

"Are you going to try to send it again?" Pete asked.

"I don't think it would do any good." Pete nodded but thankfully kept any thoughts he had to himself. Instead, he leaned against the balcony railing as well.

"Isn't it crazy how we can have fifty degree weather in February," Pete said.

"I can't say I am minding this winter being mild. The tires on my bike didn't hold up so well in the snow." Logan was a small town but steep hills made having only a bike challenging.

"I suppose they didn't," Pete agreed.

"Are you going to ask that Wendy girl to the Valentine dance?" Isaiah asked. His friend had shown a special interest in one of the girls in their ward though as far as Isaiah could tell the girl had no idea Pete even existed.

"I don't know. I want to get to know her better but I am not really in a position to date anyone seriously," Pete said. Isaiah nodded in agreement. Pete had let him crash at his small single bedroom and single bathroom apartment but it wasn't the place a man brought a woman he was courting. It was a bachelor pad from the boxes of pizza in the refrigerator to the hampers of clean yet unfolded laundry.

"Maybe meeting the right women will encourage you to get your life in order," Isaiah said.

"Could be," Pete said but he didn't sound convinced.

Silence hung between them for several long moments before Pete said "I think I am going back to bed."

"Will you throw away that letter for me?"

"I can do that," Pete said. He gave Isaiah a pat on the shoulder before leaving him to the silence of the night.

"I miss you," Isaiah said looking up at the stars. When he was a little boy his mother had always told him that no matter how far apart they were they would always be looking up at the same night sky. She might even be looking up at the stars with him that very moment and he wasn't sure if that soothed or broke his heart.

He was a man without a family. His life was not the life he had imagined he would have after his mission. Then again, his mission hadn't gone as planned either. Nothing in his life seemed to be going as he planned.

He wondered fleetingly if this time the return to sender notice on his letter had been written in his mother's tight cursive or his father's scrawling print.

It didn't really matter which had written it this time or which would send it next time. Whenever he moved to a new place he dutifully sent a letter back home. If his parents ever wanted to contact him, he wanted to make sure he had done all he could to let them know where he was. Likely though, they didn't care. They had forced him to chose between them and his faith. They had not liked the choice he had ultimately made.

Dawn followed Julie into the kitchen where the smell of cooking breakfast tantalized her nose. Denny was at the table behind an electric grill where bacon sizzled and pancakes bubbled.

Xander, his mobility dog, lay at his side on the floor waiting to be called to action.

"That smells good," Julie said stepping forward to kiss her husband on the cheek.

Denny smiled widely at her. His dark hair was in a traditional military haircut though stubble on his face said he had not yet shaved that morning. Even beneath the stubble there were signs of scars from the explosion. He had not been horrifically deformed and many women would still have considered his face handsome but it was just another sign he wore on his flesh of the sacrifice he had made for his country.

Muscled arms wrapped around Julie's waist and Dawn felt a moment of envy. No one who had seen Denny and Julie together could ever doubt the love they had for each other. It was the love she had dreamed of having with Ben.

"I have a surprise for you," Denny said to Julie. He picked up a piece of paper and handed it to her.

"A weekend getaway?" Julie asked.

"Hard to say when we will have time for another one. Especially if..." his voice trailed off and Dawn saw him give her a quick glance.

"I already told her we were seeing the fertility

specialist," Julie said. Relief showed on Denny's face. Apparently he hadn't wanted to spoil his wife's surprise.

"Once the baby comes it will be much harder to get away," Denny said.

"Oh I don't know about that. I imagine there will be grandparents fighting for the privilege of having the baby for a weekend," Julie said.

"Auntie Dawn will be fighting for that privilege as well," Dawn added.

"Still, it is Valentine's weekend," Denny said.

"It is," Julie agreed.

"The church is having a Valentine dance that weekend for singles so I figured that Dawn would have plans," Denny said.

"I hadn't planned on going," Dawn said.

Julie reached out a hand and squeezed her shoulder.

"You should go. It might be just the opportunity you need," Julie said.

"Maybe I will," Dawn conceded. Perhaps the man she was supposed to marry would be at the dance. She had met Ben at a dance shortly after he had gotten off of his mission. Dances were certainly easier than meeting men online or even at single adult activities which she didn't make it to regularly because of her busy work and school schedule.

Chapter 2

Isaiah leaned forward to look over the specs of the pedal operated clothes washer. He knew he should have it memorized by now but he didn't. In fact, he didn't have any of the specs memorized.

"I would say you can clean about five shirts at a time," Isaiah said.

"And will it clean as well as a regular washer does?" the woman asked.

"I've never personally used it," Isaiah confessed. The woman ran her hands over the floor model again and bit her lip.

"It seems expensive for a camping trip," the woman said.

"Wouldn't a laundry mat be a better option for a camping trip?" Isaiah asked.

"I have a baby in cloth diapers and we will be out in the middle of nowhere," the woman said. She put a hand on her hip.

"I have heard good things about it," Isaiah said weakly. The woman looked at the price tag and then looked at the washer again.

"I think I will talk to my husband about it," she said.

"That is probably best," Isaiah said. He watched her walk out of the door and he sighed. He walked behind the counter and picked up the product information sheet. He tried to memorize it but the information just wouldn't stay in his mind.

He looked up when the bell above the door rung again.

Pete walked up the counter and tossed a thrift store bag to him. Isaiah looked inside. He was not thrilled to see a striped suit.

"Wendy agreed to meet me at the dance. I need you to come too," Pete said.

"You need a wingman?" Isaiah asked.

"More like a chaperone," Pete said.

"Chaperone? Don't you think you are a bit old to need one of those?" Isaiah asked.

"Fine, then come as moral support. You should be getting out more anyways. There are plenty of girls at these dances. If you met someone too we could double date," Pete said.

"I am not really in a position to date anyone," Isaiah said.

"I am going to tell you what you told me. Maybe if you met the right person that would encourage you to get your life in order," Pete said.

Isaiah threw up his hands. "Sure, I will go with you. I don't have anything better to do."

He didn't have anything better to do and it might be a nice way to meet other members of the stake. He was friendly with the people in their ward but he hadn't been in Ohio long enough to attend many stake activities. At the least he might meet another returned missionary whose couch he could crash on once Pete found a girl to marry.

He really did believe that the love of a good woman

would make Pete shape up but that advice wouldn't work for him. Pete was healthy and would be a good husband if he could just focus more on his career and his cleanliness. It wasn't so easy for Isaiah.

"Father, please help me to have an open mind and an open heart as I go into this dance tonight. Please have the Holy Spirit guide me and if there is a man here who would be a good eternal companion for me please let me find him," Dawn prayed.

Julie had gone with her to the mall where she had bought a new dress for the occasion. It was turquoise with sparkles on the bodice. The flow of the dress was wavy enough that it whooshed and whirled around her as she walked. She had also gotten a new pair of shoes. They were flats and a few shades darker than the dress.

It was her commitment to putting herself back on the dating circuit.

After Julie and Denny had left for their weekend retreat she had taken the time to do her hair and makeup. She had been excited to look in the mirror and see how pretty she looked. She didn't remember the last time she had taken such care in her grooming. She was feeling excited about the new beginning in her dating life. Then, she had arrived at the dance and all the feelings of excitement faded.

This was the first time she had been at a dance alone. Before there had always been female friends to join her or Ben once they were dating. Now, she was in the parking lot alone praying for Heavenly Father's assistance.

Trembling, she opened the door and slid out of her car. She walked through the front doors, hung up her coat, and made her way to the gym which was decorated in hearts. At one end was a sound system complete with DJ. On the opposite end of the gym was a refreshment table. Along three of the four walls were chairs for sitting between dances. A line dance was playing when she entered and she did not feel up to jumping into that so she went to the refreshment table to have a cup of punch and a cookie. Then, she took a seat in one of the chairs around the dance floor.

"Dawn?" She looked across the room to where the familiar voice was coming from. Todd made his way across the room to her.

"How are you?" she asked. She stood and gave him a hug. She and Julie had gone on double dates with Ben and Todd up until Ben left the church. In fact, they had been on a double date the day that Julie got news that Denny had been injured.

Todd had broken up with Julie at a church dance leaving an opening for Denny to swoop in and make her his wife. It had been for the best. Denny and Julie were a much better couple than Todd and Julie had been.

"Would you like to dance during the next song?" Todd asked.

"Sure," Dawn said. It would be a nice retreat. The last notes of the line dance played and a slow song came on. Couples replaced the line dancers on the dance floor.

"How have you been?" Todd asked taking her hand to dance. The song was one that she had heard before but she didn't know the words to.

"Not bad," Dawn said.

"How is Julie? Is she happy?" Todd asked.

"Very," Dawn said.

"I am glad of it," Todd said and she really believed him. Todd was a good guy but he just wasn't the right guy for Julie and had never been.

"How are you?" Dawn asked. She hadn't had many opportunities to talk to Todd. Even if she had, she wasn't sure she would have taken them. He reminded her too much of Ben and the times they had enjoyed together.

"Good enough," Todd said with a shrug.

"In college?" Dawn asked. Last she had heard he was thinking about starting college. It had seemed as if he never was going to move on from his glory days as a missionary.

"Not yet."

"Are you seeing anyone?" Dawn asked.

"No. Are you?" Todd asked. She saw a sudden glimmer of hope in his eyes.

"No," Dawn said.

"Would you like to go out with me on a date or two? I am still looking for my eternal companion," Todd said. The part of her that had promised to be open minded mulled over the offer but she knew right away that she and Todd could never make a happy life together.

"You are a good guy Todd but you aren't the one for me. I don't want to waste your time," Dawn said. It was similar to what Todd had said when she broke up with Julie. She didn't want to waste his time when she knew that there was no chance she would ever end up married to Todd. He had a good heart and an honest testimony but he also was not moving forward with his life and she didn't want to be stuck with someone who was languishing in his past glories instead of working on future ones.

"Thank you for your honesty," Todd said stiffly. He finished the dance with her then walked her back to her chair. She sighed as she returned to her seat. At least she had managed to have one nice dance.

"Would you like to dance?" The voice startled her and she looked up. The gentleman asking was tall, thin, and lanky. His teeth looked like they could have used orthodontic care they had never received. Immediately, she felt repulsed but she tried to check herself. It was not fair to judge anyone on how they looked and she was there to dance.

"Yes, thank you."

He led her out to the floor and put one hand on her waist. The hand that held hers was sweaty.

"I don't believe we have met," Dawn said after what seemed like a long silence.

"I'm John Doe," he said.

"For real?" Dawn asked. She could not imagine a mother naming her child John Doe but then again in her work she had seen some unusual names and knew it was always possible.

"Not yet. I plan to change my name to John Doe and then I plan to have a son and name him John Doe two," he said. Dawn couldn't tell whether or not he was joking though he was smiling widely.

"I'm Dawn," she said. She didn't feel the need to add that Dawn was the name she had been given at birth.

"Dawn Doe. It has kind of a nice ring to it," he said. She didn't think so but it didn't seem like the polite thing to say.

"What do you do?" Dawn asked. She couldn't think of any other question to ask and she didn't think she wanted to continue to discuss names, particularly hers matched with his.

"I work for the electric company," he said. She wondered if his exposure to electricity had somehow short circuited his brain though she knew that was not a kind thought.

"How nice. Do you enjoy your work?" she asked.

"Not really. I'm just working there until my brother starts his own company."

"What does your brother want to do?" Dawn asked. One of the things she most admired about Denny was his passion for helping the deaf. She still was not certain what her own passion was but she could respect a man chasing his dreams.

"He wants to open up a pet cemetery with taxidermy services. We can bury your pets or we can stuff them so you can keep Fifi in the living room," he said. She really hoped he was joking but she didn't think so.

"How interesting," Dawn said. She was relieved when the song ended and he took her back to her seat.

"Can I give you my number?" he asked as she took her seat.

"Thanks but I don't think we would be a good fit. I

have allergies and I just think that a boyfriend who came home covered in animal fur wouldn't work," Dawn said. It was a lie but she just couldn't help herself. She didn't want to be unkind but there was no way she was going to spend any more time with John Doe nor was there any chance of her becoming Sister Doe.

"Oh, that wouldn't work," he said with a frown. He sighed and wandered away towards another girl who was seated and looking longingly to the dance floor. Perhaps he would find some woman who thought that having her deceased pet stuffed was a wonderful tribute to its life.

She sat out one more line dance and a fast song. Then, the first beats of *Can You Feel the Love Tonight* from *Disney's Lion King* began to play.

"Would you like to dance?" The man asking was a bit older than she was. He had movie star good looks with blond hair and blue eyes.

Her heart beat fast at the sight of him and she felt her mouth go dry. She hadn't felt that kind of spark since Ben.

He led her out to the dance floor and she could feel her skin tingle where his hand connected to hers. Could this be the man she was praying for? She could see spending her life with someone like him. They would certainly make beautiful babies. Her blond hair was a few shades darker than his and her eyes were hazel but she thought for sure that if they had babies together those babies could have careers in Hollywood.

"I'm Max," he said.

"Dawn," she said.

"Nice to meet you. Is this your first dance?"

"No but I haven't been to one for a while," Dawn confessed. Maybe she should have been going to dances. Maybe if she had been going to dances she would have met Max already and completely forgotten Ben's betrayal.

"Why is that?" he asked.

"I've been busy. College and work," Dawn said with a shrug.

"What do you do?" Max asked.

"I am a hospital operator," Dawn said.

"Is that what you are going to school for?" Max asked. Dawn couldn't suppress a giggle. She wasn't sure if he really thought that there was a college degree for switchboard operators or if he was just teasing her.

"I am majoring in English."

"I am a history major myself. Why did you choose English?" Max asked.

"Mostly because of my mother," Dawn said.

"Is she and English Professor?"

"No. She wanted to be a writer. She really loved books. She died of cancer when I was young," Dawn said. She felt a bit awkward sharing such a personal thing with a stranger but it felt nice to talk to Max. It had been so long since she had talked to a man she could see herself dating.

"Bummer," he said.

"Is this your first dance?" she asked. It was the only thing she could think. Being near him made her brain feel muddled.

"This is my first dance of this kind."

"What do you mean?"

"A Mormon dance. It is kind of weird. This is the first

party I have gone to in forever that didn't have smokes and booze. You guys are really serious about that whole Word of Wisdom thing aren't you?"

"You aren't a member of the church?" Dawn asked. She felt her heart sink.

"Nope. Just here with some friends," Max said. "Never really was all that big on God but heard these were great places to pick up girls."

"Your friend told you wrong," Dawn said.

"You really wouldn't date a guy like me?" He flashed her the kind of smile that made a girls knees tremble.

"No, I wouldn't," Dawn said and she knew it was true. Max might be making her heart beat a mile a minute but he certainly was not husband material.

"It is a shame. Guys like me are more fun than the guys around here," he said glancing around the room.

She wasn't sure he was wrong but she wasn't about to say so. Fun or not, she vowed to return to her chair as soon as the dance was over.

Isaiah hadn't been to a dance in ages and Pete had left him as soon as they walked through the door. He envied the women who could take a seat and observe the surroundings without being pressured to dance.

He looked around the room and decided his first dance of the evening would be a girl in a red dress who had just been returned to her seat by a man ten times better looking than him.

He wasn't in the market for a wife and a woman like her wouldn't be interested in him. It seemed like a safe choice for a dance.

He went over and asked her for a dance. He was almost surprised when she agreed.

He led her out to the dance floor. He noticed how her hand on his shoulder squeezed him just a bit unnecessarily. He guessed she was feeling for his garments. He had heard of women doing that but had never actually been on the receiving end of such an affront.

"Are you a returned missionary?" she asked. He was surprised by her bluntness.

"I am," he said.

"Where did you serve?"

"In California," he said. She looked unimpressed. He didn't dare add that he hadn't finished his mission and had been sent home early. She might walk right off the dance floor.

"Do you want a large family?"

"I suppose I am open to whatever God gives me but I never really thought about it," he said.

"What work do you do?"

"I work at a retail store. I sell simple living items. Mostly things like manual clothes washers and solar water heaters."

"Oh. Do you like the homesteading life?"

"I've thought about building one of those hobbit houses in the side of a hill. I am sure you have seen them on social media. I figured I could have solar paneling and rain water. Would be inexpensive living which would be a nice option since I am paid on commission and sadly there aren't as many simple living people in Ohio as one might expect," Isaiah said. He didn't know if she could tell he was joking or not. Either way she stopped shooting questions at him and seemed eager to return to her chair after the dance ended.

He looked around the room for the next girl he could offer a dance to. A girl in blue was being returned to her chair by a man who looked like he could have made a living in Hollywood. The girl however did not look as if she was being taken in by his charms. He wondered if the idiot had tried to get fresh with her. Too many of the men forgot that they were priesthood holders when they found themselves near beautiful women.

He walked over to her and asked for a dance. She looked tired and he wondered for a moment if she would shoo him away. Instead, she nodded and allowed him to lead her onto the dance floor.

"You look as if the night hasn't been all you hoped it would," Isaiah said softly.

"I haven't been to one of these for a while," she said.

"Neither have I," Isaiah admitted.

"I'd forgotten how varied the company can get," Dawn said.

"I think I did as well. I just had a dance that felt like an interview," Isaiah said.

"And I apparently am attracting all the oddballs tonight," Dawn said though it was more to herself than to him.

"You will be very disappointed to find that I am not an oddball. It seems I won't be much entertainment for you tonight compared to your other dancing partners. I will however tell you that you look lovely," Isaiah said. It was forward but it was also true. More importantly, it seemed like she needed to hear it.

"Thank you. I think you will be my last dance tonight," she said. She would likely be his as well though he wasn't about to say it. Already, he was feeling fatigued. He could feel the tightness in his chest and he knew that soon he would be short of breath. He hoped he could get her back to her chair before he started gasping. He had hoped to have more stamina at the dance. He thought he had been doing better but apparently tonight his body would not withstand the toil of dancing with pretty young ladies. Perhaps if he hadn't worked that morning there would have been energy to spare. Certainly, he had once been strong and healthy enough to work all day and dance all evening. Not now though.

"I didn't catch your name," Isaiah said.

"Dawn."

"It is a pleasure to meet you Dawn. I am Isaiah."

He could feel the tightness in his lungs and knew that continuing to dance and talk was more than his body could handle. Instead, he just took in the softness of her hand in his as they moved to the music. When the dance ended he returned her to her chair. He was pleased to see that she looked happier than when he had first asked her to dance.

"Have a good evening," he said. He gave her the best smile he could muster which was a bit weak. She waved goodbye as he tried to discreetly walk to the door. He made his way out to Pete's car in the parking lot. He tried the door and was relieved to find it unlocked. He sat down in the front seat and tried to take a deep breath.

He knew he should just be grateful to be alive but some days the fatigue, difficulty breathing, and pain were overwhelming. The doctors said that his symptoms could last for years or even for his entire lifetime.

He wondered if either woman had noticed the scar on his neck. The light was dim enough that they probably hadn't. Looking in the rear view mirror he could see it. He supposed his attention was most drawn to it when breathing was difficult. When he was attached to the ventilator at least he had been assured of each breath. So far, he had always managed to catch his breath once he stopped exerting himself but the feeling of suffocation always made him wonder if someday he wouldn't be able to catch his breath. He should have known better than to go to the dance and to try to dance but he just couldn't help himself. He wanted to feel normal again. Even though he wasn't.

Dawn was glad that no one else asked her to dance. After thirty minutes of sitting along the back wall she headed out to her car. The man she had danced with earlier, Isaiah, was sleeping in the passenger seat of a nearby car.

He wasn't as good looking as Max but he was not unattractive either. He had short brown hair and a slim build. At first glance he looked like a stereotypical returned missionary.

She was tempted to knock on his window and make sure he was well but she decided against it. He probably had just grown bored and decided to wait for his ride outside.

She climbed into her car and leaned her head against the headrest. Coming to the dance had been a mistake. Ben might have married and moved on with his life but she just didn't feel like she was ready to do the same.

She drove home in the dimness of the moonlight and let herself into the empty house.

She changed out of her dress and into her pajamas before climbing into bed and taking a book off the nightstand. Books were easy. People were hard. Especially boy people. She wished her love story could have been as easy as Julie's. She wished that she had a childhood best friend who could turn out to be the man of her dreams. Sadly, the men she had known in high school had ultimately let her down in much the same ways Ben had. She just wanted to meet someone she could trust. She wanted a man who was devoted to God and her. It did not seem like too much to ask.

Chapter 3

By Monday Isaiah was feeling recovered from the exhaustion of the dance. He locked his bike and walked into work ready to start his day. He punched the time clock and opened up his work email. His boss had sent him an urgent message to go to his office immediately upon arrival.

"You wanted to see me?" Isaiah asked as he opened the door to Bob's office.

"Have a seat," Bob said motioning to one of the two plush chairs across from his desk. Isaiah's stomach felt like icicles as he sat where indicated.

"I've been looking over these sales figures. Did you know you have been the lowest seller for the past three months?"

"Yes," Isaiah admitted with a sigh.

"You know what the trouble is? I can tell you. You lack passion. I can see as plain as day that you don't really have any interest in sales. I've watched you on the floor. You stop pushing at even the slightest resistance. That isn't the way to make money."

"I know," Isaiah said. He had been sure he would be good at sales. When he was a missionary he had been enthusiastic about spreading the gospel but somehow getting people to love the church was much different than convincing people to buy products, even products he believed in. Bob's simple living store had many amazing items to help people live simpler lives. They were high quality and if Isaiah had been able to afford them he would have considered taking a few home. Yet, he couldn't seem to sell them.

"Maybe with more time-"

"You just don't have it in you, kid. I'm sorry but I have to let you go."

"Let me go?"

"I'm firing you. Believe me; this is for your own good as much as mine. I'll mail you your last check. Is the address on Cherry Street still good?"

"No. I'll need to give you another," Isaiah said. Bob slid a pen and paper across the mahogany desk and Isaiah took the pen. It took him a moment to remember Pete's address. Moving around so much in such a short amount of time blended the addresses in his head.

Isaiah handed him back the paper and stood up. He reached out a hand to shake Bob's.

Then, he walked out the door to the bike rack. He undid the chain on his bike. He put on his helmet before taking off down the road. He tried to watch for signs indicating places were hiring as he slowly pedaled the two miles to Pete's apartment but he didn't see any.

His body ached as he arrived home but that happened everyday. He had to keep pushing himself. If he didn't how could he ever get better?

He carried his bike up the stairs to the second story balcony. He chained it before he let himself inside. Pete was at work so Isaiah laid down on the futon he was using as a bed and pulled out his scriptures. He opened up to where his bookmark was and began to read Isaiah chapter 41.

As a boy he had always liked the book of Isaiah if only because he shared its name but chapter 41 had not really stood out to him until he was in the hospital bed in California recovering from botulism. He had been six months into his mission.

His nurse there, Betsy, wasn't Mormon but she was a deeply devout Catholic who had studied the bible vigorously. One day, with his IV and medications, she had brought him a note that read:

Fear though not: for I am with thee: be not dismayed: for I am thy God: I will strengthen thee; yea, I will help thee: yea, I will uphold thee with the right hand of my righteousness. Isaiah 41:10

He had read the chapter, hoping to find strength and answers. He liked that verse but he found another in the chapter that he liked even more.

When the poor and needy seek water, and there is none, and their tongue faileth for thirst, I the Lord will hear them, I the God of Israel will not forsake them.

It had been reassuring to know that even when the children of Israel's tongues failed from thirst God still heard them and didn't forsake them. In the first few weeks after he was hospitalized he had difficulty breathing and a tracheotomy had been performed on him. He had been unable to speak for several days following the procedure but he had kept praying in his thoughts.

"I just want to understand. I want to know what I am

supposed to do," he whispered. It seemed simple for people like Jonah who were told exactly what God intended for them. Isaiah had heard God calling him to a mission but then on the mission he had nearly died from botulism and been sent home. He had used most of his savings to go on his mission and the remainder had been used for medical bills. Had he been wrong about being called on a mission? He wished his Patriarchal Blessing had been less vague. It had said that he would share the gospel and help those within and without the church but it had never spelled out that he was supposed to go on a mission. He had taken that for granted.

Mostly, his blessing had been about God knowing his heart and understanding all he had given up for the gospel. The blessing promised that he would be rewarded for his faith. At the moment, he would have taken a body that wasn't damaged from botulism, a job that paid a living wage, and a place to call his own.

He heard the door open and he looked up to see Pete coming through.

"You are home early," Pete said.

"Yeah. I got fired."

"Again?"

"Yeah," Isaiah said with a sigh. Since his mission he hadn't had much luck keeping any job. He had hoped the sales job would be one he could excel at.

"Do you want me to call my dad? He is the Reynoldsburg ward employment specialist. Maybe he has some leads."

"I suppose you could give him a call. I was going to

get online to see what I could find but I feel like I have applied just about everywhere in town and three jobs in the last year isn't looking very good on my applications. I might not even get any more call backs at this point," Isaiah said with a sigh and then cringed. He had to get a call back. He had no other choice. His family had disowned him when he joined the church. If he didn't find a job he would be at the mercy of the kindness of friends and the church and he didn't want that. He had to believe that God would provide. Somehow.

Chapter 4

Dawn looked at the caller id on her cell phone before answering. She was in the middle of writing a paper contrasting the experiences of Jane Austen's characters and those of Charles Dickens. Her eyes had begun to blur from staring at the screen. The call would be a welcome break.

"Hi dad." Since moving to Colorado her dad had made it a habit to call her once a week.

"Hi pumpkin. How are things going?"

"Pretty good."

"Grades where they need to be?"

"Yup." She had managed to remain a B student even with her busy work schedule. It was something she was very proud of. She had graduated high school with honors and through the first two years of college she had maintained a 4.0 GPA but as the classes had become more challenging her grades had slipped a letter. Still, it was passing and adequate to graduate.

"You let us know when graduation is. We all want to be there," he said. She felt a pang of sadness. She missed her family.

"I will."

"Wilma and I just finished unpacking."

"It is about time." Her father, his wife Wilma, and her brother Kyle had moved to Colorado a year before. They had wanted her to join them and she had used school as an excuse to stay in Ohio. While school was a legitimate reason it was not the only reason. Colorado was a nice state and she had spent many vacations there as a child but it wasn't home to her the way Ohio was. Ohio was where she was born. It was where she had lived with her mother. It was the place her mother was buried. It was also the place that her father had met the missionaries and she had become a convert.

"We found something. I wasn't sure what to do with it but we thought we should ask you."

"What is it?" Dawn asked. Had he found some favorite childhood teddy bear that by now would be moth eaten and tattered beyond recognition?

"We found a box with your mother's notebooks." Dawn took in a deep breath. Her father continued, "Kyle doesn't want them but I can't bring myself to throw them away either. I suppose I could put them in the attic but-"

"No, I'll take them," Dawn said. Kyle was younger than her and his memories of their mother were vaguer. He didn't feel the same need to be connected to her as she did. It was true her stepmother tried hard to love them as if they were her own. Kyle had been eager to let her but it had been harder for Dawn. She had spent every waking moment for the first three years after stomach cancer claimed her mother wishing for her back.

"I'll send them out later this week."

"Thanks dad."

"We miss you. When are you coming out for a visit?"

"I'm not sure. Maybe once this term is over."

"We saved a room for in case you want to come here after you graduate," he said. Dawn smiled. She didn't want to join her family in Colorado but it was nice to know that she was missed and that they were making sure she always had a place to call home.

"Thanks. I'll keep that in mind."

"I need to go now. I love you pumpkin."

"I love you too, dad," Dawn said. She closed her phone and leaned against the wall trying to clear her head. Good sense said she should go to Colorado. Her family was there and she would have a place to live. Kyle would be leaving for his mission soon and it might be nice for her dad and stepmother to have her around. She could look for a job as easily there as she could here. Dawn sighed. Thinking about it all made her weary. She didn't feel like Colorado was calling to her but then again there was nothing else calling out to her either. There was nothing in her heart saying whether she should stay or go. There was nothing telling her what job she should get or whether she should go on a mission once college was over. She didn't feel particularly called to serve but at the same time she wasn't feeling a strong pull anywhere else either. At least with a mission God could tell her exactly where he wanted her. She wanted to put it in his hands. It was too hard holding it in her own.

The office Isaiah walked into was neat and well kept. It was a strong contrast to how Pete kept his own space.

"Brother Campbell?"

"Please, call me Jonas."

"Isaiah." He reached out to shake Jonas's hand. Jonas looked about twenty ears older than him. He had crew cut brown hair and a scar that ran down the side of his neck and into his collar. He had the same nose as Pete and a similar eye color but that was where the similarities ended. Pete was thin and intellectual but Jonas gave the impression of being a man's man.

"Pete told me a bit about your predicament but I want to hear it from you."

"I've had three jobs in the last year. I started doing factory work but I got fired because I couldn't keep up. I thought it must just be the after affects of the botulism."

"Pete mentioned you had been sent home from your mission due to illness."

"Yes sir. So after I was fired at the factory I got a job answering phones for a contractor. They let me go after sixty days. They said I didn't have the skills they were looking for after all. I ended up working retail. Apparently, I am not a particularly good salesman either."

"What did you do before your mission? Did you work?"

"Mostly handyman jobs. My father was a Baptist pastor. We lived in a small community that was fairly poor. Many of the congregants were elderly so we were often called to fix leaks, paint houses, or repair fencing. I didn't have a real job. My father assumed I would go to college for a theology degree. I probably would have too if I hadn't found the church." He pushed away the pain that talking about his family always gave him. He had loved his father and perhaps even idolized him. They had spent so much of his youth working side by side. Now, his father wouldn't even accept his letters.

"What is it you think you want to do?" Isaiah took a

moment before he answered. He knew it was important to be honest but the honest answer wasn't very helpful.

"I don't know."

"Did you like the handyman work?"

"I liked helping people. I didn't mind the work though I probably would be slower at it these days. I get fatigued much easier now than I did before. Any jobs would have to be nearby. I don't have a car and these days I can only bike about five miles before I start to wear out. On my mission we were doing fifteen miles a day easy. "

Jonas sat silently for a moment while tapping his pen on the desk. Isaiah wondered if Jonas thought it was as hopeless as he did. He wanted to work but the jobs he was qualified to do were ones that his illness made difficult.

"I have a friend who might have some temporary handyman work. He won't mind if you are a bit slow as long as you do good work. Let me make some calls. It won't be a permanent solution. We will need to try to find you something else to do."

"I appreciate it," Isaiah said. He stood up and pushed in his chair.

"One more thing. This is as a father of a son and as a friend. Start fasting and praying for direction. If I put you in a job that isn't right for you we will be back here in another four months. If you have an idea of where you want to go and what you want to do I can help you much more easily."

"Thanks."

Isaiah didn't add that he had been fasting and praying already. He had even been delving into his scriptures half an hour each day before searching online for jobs. Still, he wasn't feeling any guidance from the Spirit. He cringed at the thought. He hadn't heard the Spirit loud and clear since before the fateful day at the ward potluck that had ended his mission. While he was in the hospital he had asked God again and again why the Spirit didn't warn him about the potato salad. He was on his mission. He was doing everything he was supposed to do. Other missionaries took their missions more lightly. He knew one set of Elders who frequently went to a particular member's house to play video games even though it was against the rules. He had also had one companion who had been carrying on inappropriately with a sister missionary and gotten both of them sent home. Isaiah wasn't like that. He wanted to spread the Gospel. He wanted to bring as many people to Christ as he could. Yet, he was one of only three people who had eaten the bad potato salad at the ward potluck and of those exposed to the toxin he had gotten the sickest. It didn't make sense to him. Why had God allowed things to happen that way?

Dawn looked up from the stove where she was browning ground beef for tacos as Denny wheeled himself into the dining room followed by Xander. Julie joined them a moment later. In her arms was a white bag with the logo of a local pharmacy.

"Need any help?" Julie asked as she sat the bag down on the counter.

"I've got it," Dawn said. Julie opened the bag and took out several orange medicine bottles. She slipped them into the cupboard. Julie and Denny had their own bathroom however it lacked a medicine cabinet. A towel rack and a medicine cabinet were some of the small improvements Denny had plans to make but could more easily do with help from his father or father-in-law. Since all three men worked long hours anything not essential was usually left for later.

"Tomorrow night we will be having a guest for dinner," Julie said.

"Who?" Dawn asked. Julie and Denny's family often came over for dinner but they weren't considered guests and their appearance at dinner wasn't something that would usually warrant mentioning.

"A returned missionary named Isaiah."

"You aren't trying to set me up, are you?" Dawn asked. She felt a tightening in her stomach. A blind date was the last thing she needed.

"Nothing like that. It is a favor to a friend. Do you remember Jonas, the employment specialist from Reynoldsburg ward who helped me look into interpretive apprenticeships? The former marine."

"Only vaguely," Dawn admitted.

"He called me today. Apparently Isaiah is a friend of his son. He got sick while serving a mission and has been having trouble keeping a job since. He has a background as a handyman so Jonas thought I might be able to give him some work around here. Jonas is worried that this guy is feeling guilty about being sent home from his mission. Maybe his self esteem is suffering a bit. Jonas is hoping that with some honest work we can help him get back on his feet. I guess he also has some lingering effects from his illness. It will be good for Jonas to gauge Isaiah's physical limitations before trying to find him a job. I guess he figured that since I know a thing or two about physical limitations I would be patient." Denny smiled. Sometimes it was easy to forget that Denny did indeed have physical limitations.

Denny had a modified car so he could drive himself wherever he needed to go. The house had been specially modified to meet his needs and within it Denny was independent. Outside their home Xander helped Denny with many tasks but that didn't mean that Denny never faced challenges.

"What kind of work will you have him do?" Julie asked. She closed the cupboard and sat down at the table. Dawn added the seasoning mix to the meat and opened the refrigerator to take out the sour cream, shredded cheese, tortillas, lettuce, and sliced tomatoes.

"I don't completely know yet."

"I could finally get that medicine cabinet," Julie said. "I know just the one I want. I saw it in a magazine. Tessa always brings in those homemaking magazines and we were slow so I got a chance to look at it. Anyways, it is the cutest thing. It has a square mirror with grid work designs decorating it. Underneath the mirror are these three little shelves. The whole thing is white and would match really well with the vanity I want to put in," Julie said. Dawn smiled at her. Her geeky friend was never the type of person she pegged as a homemaker. Julie was the type of girl who would have been at home at a comic con or a sci fi convention. She had never paid much attention to fashion and was more likely to read Wizard than Good Housekeeping. However, since she had moved into her own home she had become obsessed with making it both practical and beautiful.

"We can see if he is up to those things. I think we will start him off a bit smaller though until we know what he can handle. There is the towel rack in the bathroom that I haven't hung up yet. I suppose a new coat of paint wouldn't hurt around here either. Plus, you said you wanted new wallpaper in the bathrooms. I'm sure we can find projects to keep him busy. Especially if he tires easy. Who knows how long those tasks will take him."

"Have you met him yet?"

"No."

"Any idea what kind of foods our guest enjoys?" Julie asked.

"We can just do a cookout. There will be plenty of options and I have yet to meet anyone who couldn't find something to eat at a cookout. I'll have my parents over as well so there won't be any pressure on him and we can get to know him."

"I think you are just looking for an excuse to grill," Julie said with a laugh.

"Maybe just a bit," Denny said. He reached out and took Julie's hand in his and Dawn busied herself with pouring the taco meat into a serving dish. Denny. If Ben had made different choices it could have been him and her holding hands over a plate of taco shells in the kitchen of their own home. It could have been him and her trying to have a baby.

"I will never forgive my father for getting you that grill as a wedding present," Julie said with a laugh.

"Dawn, help me out here, don't I make a great burger?"

"He does," Dawn agreed forcing a smile. She was glad that Julie and Denny had found love together but sometimes she felt like a third wheel. No home was really big enough for a newly wed couple, a dog, and a roommate.

Chapter 5

Isaiah was sure he had the wrong house. This house was in a nice area of Lancaster. It wasn't the wealthiest area where doctors, lawyers, and CEOs resided but it was in a modest neighborhood. All the lawns on the street were neatly mowed. Many had flower gardens and ornaments in the front. The house across the street had a white picket fence that had a trellis instead of a gate as entryway.

The house before him was red brick with a gabled roof. Though the house did look older the bricks were in good shape. It didn't look like the house needed any repairs to it and surely the owners could afford a trained handyman if they could afford to live in such a nice area. He turned around but Pete had already taken off down the road.

Cautiously, he knocked.

He tried not to show his surprise when the door was answered by a man in a wheelchair. A bright eyed golden retriever stood by his side.

"You must be Isaiah," he said.

"And you must be Denny Miller."

"And this is Xander," Denny indicated the dog at his side. "He is off duty right now so you can pet him if you want to."

Isaiah reached out and let Xander sniff his hand for a moment before reaching behind his ear and beginning to rub. Xander wagged his tail enthusiastically at the affection.

"Brother Campbell said you had some work I could

help you with." Clearly, this man needed help since he was in a wheelchair and had a service dog. When Brother Campbell had sent him here he had felt like he was being thrown a bone. He thought there must be some member who felt sorry enough for him to let him while away the hours on idle tasks and pay him a passable sum. It wasn't the case. Denny Miller obviously needed his labor.

"I sure do. Won't you come in? We are having a cookout on the patio. We are supposed to get snow next week so we thought we better enjoy the warm weather while it lasts. Please, join us."

"Thanks but-"

"I insist. We have plenty of food."

"Of course," Isaiah said. He followed Denny through a well kept and tidy house. The house was U shaped with hallways going from either side of the living room where. He followed Denny straight through the living room and into an open kitchen and dining room. Against the back wall of the kitchen was a sliding glass door that opened onto the back patio. Denny gave a command and Xander pulled on a rope opening the back door. Isaiah followed him down a ramp onto a concrete slab. A grill and picnic table were set up on the concrete. An umbrella hung over the picnic table. In the summer it might add shade but it seemed laughable in February.

"These are my parents," Denny said pointing to a man and woman who smiled politely at him. Everyone was wearing turtle necks or sweaters but none had jackets on in the 55 degree weather.

"Brother and Sister Miller?"

"That's right," Sister Miller said. She was unwrapping a stack of Styrofoam plates.

"This is Julie, my lovely wife," Denny said indicating a thin woman with straight chestnut hair. She was pouring a bag of chips into a large bowl. He couldn't help think that it was good of her to stay married to her husband after whatever accident had left him in his wheelchair. He had met plenty of people in his time as a pastor's son and as a missionary who had quit when the times got hard.

"And this is Dawn. She is our roommate," Denny said indicating a woman who was opening boxes of plastic cutlery. Dawn was just inches shorter than he was. He recognized her as the girl from the dance but in the light of day he could see her more clearly than he had in the dimness of the dance floor. Her petite nose and thin lips gave her a hint of delicacy. Her smile shone in her hazel eyes.

"We have met," Dawn said giving him a smile. He smiled back at her.

"Please, have a seat," Julie said indicating a place at the picnic table. He wasn't sure what else to do so he sat down.

"Would you prefer a hamburger or hotdog?" Brother Miller asked.

"Hamburger is fine," Isaiah said. He felt his skin warm and his heart began to pulse in his head. If he was still a missionary this would have been so easy. He wasn't sure why sitting down to a meal with virtual strangers was so hard now when not long ago it had been routine.

"Are you from Ohio originally?" Denny said.

"I'm originally from Missouri."

"How did you end up here?"

"My first mission companion was from here. After I got sent home he let me come stay with him for a while. I got to know people and bounced around some. Now I am staying with Pete."

"Are your parents still in Missouri?" Sister Miller asked.

"I can't imagine them being anywhere else but I can't answer that honestly because I don't know."

"You don't know?" Sister Miller asked.

"I haven't talked to my parents since I was baptized when I turned eighteen."

"I can't imagine," Sister Miller said. She stole a glance at her son. Isaiah wondered if she would still speak to him if he ever decided to become another faith.

"An LDS family moved into our school district my freshman year. Me and their oldest boy were in shop class together and we kept getting partnered. I took that as a sign that I was supposed to try to convert him away from his faith and convince him to be saved. He had the last laugh." Mosiah had told him that if he wanted to discuss the tenants of his faith that he better understand them. Mosiah had given him a Book of Mormon to read and Isaiah had planned to read it and disprove the whole thing. Instead, the Spirit had spoken to him and he had no doubt that the Book of Mormon was just as much the word of God as the Bible. With Mosiah's help he had contacted the missionaries and used "study sessions" with Mosiah as a way to hear the discussions. He was sure he wanted to be baptized by the time he was sixteen but he had to either get his parents, who he hadn't told about his new faith, to sign or wait until he was eighteen.

He hadn't even waited a month after turning eighteen to be baptized and that night, when he told his parents, was the last time they had spoken.

He had moved in with Mosiah's family until he was ready to go on his mission but by the time he had returned their family was in turmoil. Mosiah's father had left the church as well as his marriage.

Isaiah's laugh sounded forced and afterwards a silence hung in the air. Dawn wasn't sure what to do so she reached out and grabbed the bowl nearest to her.

"Would you like some potato salad?" she asked extending the bowl to him. She was surprised when he physically recoiled. His face turned ashen and his fingers flew to the base of his neck.

"No. Thank you," he said but it seemed as if he was forcing the words out. She pulled the bowl away from him quickly.

Everyone sat around the table awkwardly for a moment. She guessed that they, like her, were trying to figure out what they should say. Finally, Julie broke the silence.

"Is everything alright? Do you have a food allergy? I'm so sorry that we didn't know." Julie's voice was soft and calm. It was the same voice Dawn had heard her use sometimes on disoriented dementia patients who she was trying to register.

"I'm sorry," Isaiah said. His cheeks turned pink and he looked as if he was hoping that the house would catch fire or perhaps that an asteroid would fall from the sky and leave a giant crater on the patio to distract the attention from him. She couldn't help feeling embarrassed for him.

"It is alright," Julie said soothingly. "I suppose I should have consulted you about the food we were serving."

"It was unusual circumstances. This potato salad probably came from the store," Isaiah said though it seemed more to himself than to them.

"It did. I'm afraid that I don't have much time to make homemade foods," Julie said. Now it was her turn for flushed cheeks.

"I didn't mean anything like that. I'm being a terrible guest. I apologize. Potato salad was the reason I was sent home from my mission. I guess I should explain. It is such a strange story," Isaiah said.

"I work in healthcare and I have heard some unusual stories before. I would like to hear yours," Dawn said. She couldn't help finding herself fascinated by him as he squirmed and then gave a sigh as if he had needed to build up his courage before speaking. He didn't have any of the confidence he had exhibited when they had danced and she couldn't imagine any story involving potato salad causing someone so much distress.

"When I was on my mission in California there were many families who were homesteading. They were attempting to live off the land and be as natural as possible. One family had a huge garden and they stored many of their vegetables by canning. They had never canned potatoes before but the Sister decided to try it. She made an error somewhere along the way. There was a potluck at church and she used her canned potatoes to make a potato salad. The doctors said that if it had been a hot food it might have killed the botulism but it was a cold food and so the potatoes weren't cooked. I got really sick. I was lucky the doctors realized what it was and were able to treat me. I probably would have died otherwise," Isaiah said. If she would have read about it in a novel she wouldn't have believed it for a moment but she could tell from Isaiah's shaking hands that he was telling them the truth.

"I'm thinking less of this potato salad now myself," Julie said. She grabbed the bowl from the table and took it inside.

The table was still silent when she returned.

"I still have a hard time with loud noises," Denny said casually. Dawn was glad he had broken the silence. She had been trying to find something to say but no words were coming to her.

"Loud noises?" Isaiah asked looking confused.

"I was in the army. IED," he said indicating his chair. Isaiah nodded slowly. He seemed to realize that Denny was trying to reassure him that his awkwardness wouldn't be held against him and it wouldn't. The Miller's weren't those kinds of people and neither was she.

"I'm sorry," Isaiah said. It was what everyone always said when Denny mentioned the circumstances of his paralysis.

"Nah, don't be. Best thing that could ever have happened to me," Denny said with a smile.

Denny had to be kidding but Isaiah was glad that he was trying to make light of the situation. After all, it had taken the tension from the table after his ridiculous display of cowardice against a bowl of food. Still, he was beginning to feel antsy and ready to work. He ate his food hurriedly and then stood up to throw away his empty plate. Sister Miller smiled as she took it from him and bid him to sit back down. He did but he turned towards Denny.

"What work do you have for me to do?" Isaiah asked.

"Odds and ends mostly. I was thinking that tonight you could hang a towel rack for me in the bathroom. I've already marked the wall where the holes will need to be drilled. The drill and leveler are in the toolbox outside the bathroom."

"I can show him," Dawn offered.

"And after that?"

"Nothing else today. Tomorrow I will have you painting. My wife has promised me that she has finally settled on a paint color. I thought it would be easy. Walk in the store. Look at the color choices. Pick a color. Come home. Apparently it isn't," Denny said with a laugh.

"I needed to look at the colors against the carpet," Julie said but he could tell that there was no defensiveness there. She looked at her husband with adoration. It was a way no woman had ever looked at him.

"That is fine. I just need to let my ride know my plans," Isaiah said. Pete was being a good sport about shuttling him around but he knew that eventually he would need a better plan. There was not an active bus service in their area and Logan and Lancaster were too far apart for him to bike and would have been even if he had been in optimal health.

"Don't worry about it. I can drop you off tonight and pick you up tomorrow evening. I'll come and get you around four. My class is scheduled until four but the professor usually lets us go early." Denny said.

"Sure," Isaiah said.

He got up when Dawn did and followed her down the hallway to the door where the toolbox was waiting.

The towel rack wasn't what he had pictured. He had been picturing a single bar that would need only two screws to hold it. In actuality it was a three barred design that would hold six towels if filled to capacity. Eight screws were needed to hold it in place or so the manufacturer apparently thought. Denny had marked the top and bottom holes of the rack approximately but Isaiah still needed to mark the middle four, drill the pilot holes, and secure the rack with screws.

It took an hour and a half before he opened the bathroom door and glanced down the hallway. The lights were on in the living room so he made his way in that direction.

The older Brother and Sister Miller were gone. Denny was at the table with a text book opened in front of him. Xander was at Denny's feet. Julie was across from him glancing through a catalog.

"I'm all finished," Isaiah said.

"That's great. Let me grab my keys and I will take you home," Denny said. Isaiah followed him out to the garage. Denny opened the back door of the car and Xander took his seat.

"Do you need any help?" He asked as Denny used a board to move from his wheelchair to the driver's seat.

"I got it," Denny said folding the wheelchair down and placing it into a rack apparently made for that purpose. He pushed the garage door opener letting the fading light of sunset creep in.

Isaiah climbed into the passenger side and tried not to appear too fascinated by the levers Denny used instead of foot pedals. He wanted to ask questions but he held back. Denny Miller was being kind to him and it wouldn't be right to return that kindness with rudeness.

"That IED really was the best thing that ever happened to me. I just didn't know it at the time," Denny said as the car slowly backed out of the driveway.

Isaiah nodded. He wasn't sure what to say. He didn't see how losing the ability to walk could be the best thing that had ever happened to anyone. That would be like saying his near death by botulism was the best thing to ever have happened to him.

"When I was in the army I was engaged to be married. Her name was Shannon. She seemed like a real catch at the time. She was beautiful but also active in the church. She wanted to get married and have babies as much as I did. I thought she and I were going to have a perfect life together. Then I ended up in a wheelchair and she left me. I was without a career or the woman I had thought was going to be my eternal companion. I moved back in with my parents and things were looking pretty bleak.

What I am trying to say is that God has a plan for everything. Even when we really don't understand it.

I needed to lose everything so I could have the things I was supposed to have. If I could still walk I wouldn't be married to Julie. I don't know if you have a good woman in your life or not but losing use of my legs feels like a small price to pay for her."

"No woman in my life at the moment. I'm not really in the position to have one."

"Don't sell yourself short on that. A good woman can handle the trials that are given to us."

"Thanks for sharing," Isaiah said. He knew Denny meant well. He wondered what all Pete had told Jonas and what Jonas had in turn told Denny about him. As much as Denny was trying to help, Isaiah knew he wasn't Denny. He had sacrificed his relationships with his parents and siblings for the gospel. He had used all his college savings to go on a mission which had ended abruptly. Now, he was just trying to find a job where he wouldn't get fired and be able to afford an apartment on his own. He had to believe that with all he had sacrificed for his faith, God would at least give him that. He didn't even dare to ask for a love like the one Denny and Julie Miller clearly shared.

Chapter 6

Dawn shivered against the cold. The temperature had dropped down to the upper teens and three inches of snow covered the front lawn. She was glad the roads were clear. When she had left for work the night before they had been slick.

She opened the front door and kicked off her snow boots. She had just shrugged her coat off her shoulders and closed the door when she heard a sound. It took her a moment to figure out that it was soft sobbing. Hesitantly, she followed the noise to where Julie's bedroom door was a quarter opened and Dawn could just make out her friend lying on the bed.

"Are you alright?" Dawn asked.

Julie sat up and opened the door the rest of the way and Dawn saw that there was a box of tissues on the king size bed that was at the center of the room.

"It is just the hormones. I didn't think that the side effects from the medicines would be so rough. I hoped I could have a little cry session and get it all over with before Denny came home. It would make him feel bad if he saw me like this and you know how sensitive Xander is too." Dawn nodded. Both Denny and Xander would be upset by her tears. As a service dog Xander was more sensitive to the emotions of those around him than a pet would have been.

"How much longer do you need to take them?"

"We will be doing the implantation next week," Julie said. "The doctor is going to start us off slow. He is going to implant one egg and see if it sticks. If not he will try two next time. Denny and I told him we wouldn't go higher than two eggs because of our beliefs. Thankfully, he understood," Julie said.

"He wanted to implant more?" Dawn asked. She had heard of more than one media sensation where women had birthed litters of babies.

"He just told us it was a possible option. Sometimes couples risked implanting more eggs and if more than two babies resulted they terminated some of them," Julie said.

"How awful." Dawn tried to imagine how any woman who had desperately tried to have a baby could end the life of babies she carried. How did one choose which babies lived and which died? She supposed that must be the reason some women had such large amounts of babies on occasion. Maybe those women couldn't go through with termination.

"I need your opinion on something." Dawn hoped it had nothing to do with reproductive choices. She didn't think she could ever make the choices Julie was making. Denny and Julie were lucky. They could afford to do multiple fertility cycles. How awful it would be for people who could only do one or two cycles to have to decide if they would risk better chances of cycles working against the possibility of being forced to terminate babies if a mother couldn't carry them all safely to term.

Julie stood up and walked across the room to the computer desk and handed Dawn a paper that was in the printer tray.

Dawn took it from her and looked the paper over. Her

heart sank as she read Julie's resignation letter. It was politely written in twelve point font and it was professional without spelling or grammar errors.

"It looks fine," Dawn said.

"I know everyone will be disappointed. In a way, I am disappointed. I really love my job. I know that several women have had perfectly healthy pregnancies and still kept working but-"

"I think it is the right thing to do. Those other women didn't go through what you are. I'm sure it will be easier on your body to not work." Registrars were often on their feet and pushing a heavy cart loaded down with a computer and attached printer. If Julie was trying to get pregnant it probably wasn't the best thing for her to be doing.

"You won't be mad at me?" Julie asked. Dawn was surprised she could even think such a thing.

"How could I be? You have been there for years. Plus, it isn't as if you are just leaving without notice. You are going through the proper channels."

"Denny thought it was time. He always assumed once we had a baby I would stay home."

"Absolutely," Dawn said. If it had been her she would have wanted to stay home with a baby as well. It made her wonder if it ever would be her. Since Ben, the idea of her getting married and having babies seemed so distant. It almost felt impossible though if Julie and her paralyzed husband could believe God would someday give them a child then she had to believe the same miracle might one day be hers.

Isaiah climbed the porch and knocked on the door of the Miller house. He was glad that the path he had salted and shoveled the day before was still clear. Besides the sidewalk he had also cleared the porch. The work had worn him out and left his arms sore but it was a good kind of sore and one he had not experienced in far too long.

Beside the door was a large cardboard box. If he hadn't cleared the snow the box might have been wet and damaged but on the clear and dry porch it had avoided warping. Dawn answered his knock with a cheery smile.

"Looks like you have a box that came," Isaiah said indicating it.

"I didn't hear the delivery guy," Dawn said opening the door and hurrying over to the delivered box. He could see her eyes lit up as she looked at the label. She wrapped her arms around the box attempting to lift it and he hurried to her side.

"You should grab a coat." She had a sweater on but it would do little to protect her from the chill in the air.

"I'm fine," she said and he decided not to argue with her. He joined her in lifting the box.

It was heavier than he expected.

"You have rocks in here?" he asked teasingly. Her sparkling eyes told him that whatever was in the box was something dear to her.

"Notebooks," Dawn said as together they carried the box over the threshold. "Can you help me get it to my room?"

"Sure," Isaiah said. It took some struggling and maneuvering but they did manage to get the box inside her door.

He returned to the doorway to take off his boots and hang up his coat. By the time he came back to Dawn's room she had scissors in her hand. He watched as she fought with the packaging tape to reveal the contents of the box.

"Quite excited about those notebooks?" He couldn't imagine what anyone could need with a box that size filled with notebooks. She would have to be in college the rest of her life to use them.

"They were my mother's. She was a writer." He could tell from her tone that her mother was deceased. Either that or her mother, like his, had gone from her life and was not likely ever to come back.

"What happened to her?" He asked as gently as he could. If she didn't want to talk about it he wouldn't press her but he couldn't help being curious either.

"She had cancer."

"I'm sorry."

"I am too," Dawn said.

"What are you planning to do with all of these then?"

"I haven't a clue," Dawn admitted.

"She must have written quite a lot," Isaiah said. In all his years of schooling he had never filled up so many notebooks.

"My mom wrote her first story when she was seven. When she got really sick I spent a lot of time talking to her about her childhood. She never wanted to play outside with the other kids. She was happiest with a pen and notebook. When kids at school would tease her about being bookish she would write them in terrible roles like the princess who got eaten by the dragon. I laughed at that because I was little and didn't really understand. Now, I sometimes wish I could make people get eaten by dragons," Dawn said. He understood the sentiment.

"Was she ever published?" he asked.

"No. I don't even know if she ever tried to be. She was a wife and a mother before anything else. I think she just wrote because she loved it."

"Still, if this stuff is any good, don't you think she would have wanted people to read it?"

"I've taken several creative writing classes. Everyone says it is nearly impossible to get a publisher. I can't imagine approaching an agent and explaining that the author who wrote the books is dead. Even if they do publish her books, there won't be any more books after these."

"What about publishing them yourself?" Isaiah asked. One of the things he had learned in California was that there were many ways to be self sufficient. Plenty of artists had their own shops or sold their own work out of studios. He had even seen a group of three teenagers standing outside of a pizza parlor attempting to hand out free samples of their music to passersby. If he hadn't been on his mission he would have taken a copy just because of their enthusiasm.

Dawn looked at the notebooks before her and then up at him again.

"It is a huge undertaking. I'm not sure I could really do it."

"What if I agreed to help you?"

"You would do that?"

"I don't exactly have much else going on. Except the work around here. I could read to you and you could type, assuming you have better typing skills than I have. "

"They are so-so," Dawn admitted.

"Well then, we should be able to get through some of these."

"What if she didn't complete them?"

"Then we can do it. Didn't you ever play the game on the school playground where you told a story around the circle and everyone added on to the person before them? I was pretty good at that," Isaiah said. His mind tried to take him back to those days but he pushed the memories away. Those were people he would never see again. They were people who would likely as not spit on him now if they saw him.

"I'll make sure you have extra time," a masculine voice said. Isaiah turned to see Denny just beyond the doorway. He hadn't even heard his chair approach. Either that or his ears had been clouded by his thoughts.

"No need to make my tasks light," Isaiah said. There had been a time when he had worked from sun up to sun down with his father and never tired. He wished he could have those days back. The doctors said he might someday recover more fully but it was a matter of time and the will of God. It was hard enough to struggle with believing that God had let his mission end prematurely. It was too much for his faith to believe God was keeping him weak and sickly when others easily healed and so he pushed those thoughts away.

"It seems like a worthwhile project," Denny said. Isaiah had no idea whether Denny really believed that or not. But he did. He felt enthusiasm bubble up within him at the idea of helping Dawn bring her deceased mother's work to life.

"Why don't I go through them over the next few days and we can pick one story to start on," Dawn said. She had already pulled several onto her lap and was flipping through pages with loose cursive lettering.

"Sounds good to me," Isaiah said. He turned around and headed into the hallway with Denny and Xander.

"I have a medicine cabinet in my trunk that needs hung up. Are you up to it today?" Denny asked. Isaiah hated that his weakness was so obvious. Still, he felt determined.

"It might take some time." If he could go slowly he could complete the task. He was sure of it.

"We have plenty of that," Denny said.

Isaiah nodded. At the moment free time was one thing he had an abundance of and for probably the first time in his life he wished he didn't.

Chapter 7

"Surprise!" Dawn said lifting the lid of the box to reveal a chocolate cake with white icing covered in various healthcare symbols. The First Aid cross sat beside the Rod of Asclepius. There was also an image of a milk cow that Dawn had requested which had made the bakery staff member taking her order give her a confused look.

"I love this," Julie said with a laugh.

"I wouldn't have thought of that," another coworker said as she stepped forward to push the Computer on Wheels, the COW, out into the hallway. A patient had been brought to bed eleven and even a farewell cake could not slow down the busy ER.

"We wanted to do something special for your last day," Dawn said. It made her heart ache to think that this would be the last shift she and Julie would share. Julie would be moving on. She would be focusing all of her time and energy on making and raising a baby. Dawn really wished she knew what she was going to do with her life. In June she would graduate college but there didn't seem to be anything on the other side of that. She didn't know what job she wanted to pursue. She had thought once or twice about just staying a hospital operator. It was a good job but without Julie there she thought the job would be less fun than it once had been.

Dawn reached for the knife to cut into the cake when the code phone rang. Sighing, she stepped forward and picked up the receiver.

"Operator," she said.

"We have a code green," the nursing supervisor said.

Dawn hung up the code phone and held down the button to activate the overhead paging system.

"Attention, Code Green," Dawn said into the microphone. She heard her voice coming from the speaker down the hall. She repeated the message and then released the button and turned to Julie.

"Guess we couldn't get a break on my last night," Julie said. Dawn sighed. She had only ever had one code green before. External disasters were thankfully uncommon and the last time there had been one was when an explosion at a warehouse nearby had caused a partial roof collapse. A dozen workers were injured but thankfully there had only been one death. Dawn wondered what disaster had struck tonight.

Julie grabbed her COW and headed to the ambulance bay. Dawn watched the security cameras as the first ambulance pulled in.

Isaiah climbed out of Pete's car and walked up the sidewalk to the Miller's door. He hesitated for a moment before knocking. The only vehicle in the driveway was Denny's modified one. He pulled out his phone and checked the time. He wasn't early.

He heard the patter of dog paws as the door opened. Denny smiled at him but the smile seemed forced. Isaiah opened his mouth to apologize, wondering whether he had missed a call from Denny or misunderstood when he was expected, but Denny raised his hand.

"Julie and Dawn are on their way home. They had to

stay late. It was a bad night at work. I forgot until just a moment ago that you were coming," Denny said.

"I can call Pete and have him pick me up," Isaiah said.

"That isn't necessary. Come in and you can help me make breakfast for them," Denny said.

Within thirty minutes bacon was draining on a paper towel, muffins were cooling, and cheese was melting over eggs.

Isaiah heard a car in the driveway and headed towards the door.

Julie rushed past him and into Denny's awaiting arms. Isaiah was almost shocked to see her climb into Denny's lap and cling to him as he held her.

A moment later Dawn's car pulled in. She turned the car off and opened her door. Her eyes were red and swollen. He had no doubt she had been crying.

He wasn't sure is she would accept his comfort but he held his arms out to her and hesitantly she leaned into them. He had intended to hug her and then release her but she clung to him as fresh sobs emerged.

"What happened?" he asked.

"There was a shooting. A bad one. We got twenty patients from it and others were sent to Columbus," Dawn whispered.

"It was at candlelight vigil," Julie said. Her voice was angry across the yard. "Who kills people holding a vigil?"

"Bad people," Denny said stroking Julie's hair. Isaiah was sure Denny had known his share of bad people during his times overseas.

"I had so many families calling me tonight to try to

find out if their loved ones were there," Dawn said. "Then, the families started coming in and it was even worse. The woman they put in the room across from our work station didn't make it. For two hours I was trying to answer phones and reassure families while a mother was just outside of my door screaming 'my baby.' I have had some rough nights but this is the worst," Dawn said.

"It was awful," Julie said.

"Not a good last night," Denny said. "But you never have to go back there."

Isaiah supposed the words were comforting to Julie but he didn't know what to say to Dawn. She would have to go back unless she left her job.

"We made breakfast," he said lamely.

Dawn pulled away from him and immediately he felt a chill. He wished her warm body was still against his. It had been so long since he had been physically close to anyone. He missed the hugs his mother had given him and the cuddles his little sisters demanded. He ached for family.

"Thank you," Dawn said stepping back and wiping her eyes. He doubted she felt much like eating after such an awful night. He wouldn't.

Denny was already wheeling his chair up the ramp with Julie in his lap. Dawn fell into step behind them and Isaiah followed.

He watched Dawn step forward and grab a plate. She smiled up at him as she picked up a blueberry muffin. Her smile made his heart beat a little faster though he wasn't sure why. Dawn was his friend. She and the Miller's were good people who had been helping him.

Chapter 8

Dawn clicked the button to submit the third application she had filled out that day to the awaiting human resources department.

She had gone online searching for jobs that wanted applicants with English degrees. Some wanted a masters degree or higher. Most wanted experience. She hoped one of the employers would be willing to overlook her lack of experience and give her a chance though the rock in the pit of her stomach whispered that was unlikely.

The first day back at work after the tragedy had been difficult. Her coworkers who had missed it had wanted a rehash of the events that she hadn't felt like giving.

It had been more than a week since the shooting and it still made her sick to walk through the hospital doors and without Julie there to talk to the nights felt longer and harder. She had grown up responsibilities so she couldn't just walk away from her job but she knew that she couldn't stay at the hospital forever. She needed to find something else. She needed a fresh start.

The knock on the door drew her from her thoughts. It was about time for Isaiah to arrive. Julie and Denny were away at the doctors and so she assumed they had told him not to come.

"Hello. I won't be coming in. Denny said he was away but that I could work on the yard until he returned. I just didn't want to startle you by banging around the garage without some warning first," Isaiah said. His smile was teasing and it felt like sunshine.

"What does he have you doing?"

"Yard work. Nothing especially exciting." A warm spell the second week of March had melted the snow but she hoped it didn't get too warm. There had been plenty of springs before where flowers had bloomed prematurely only to be taken down by unexpected frosts. Ohio weather was utterly unpredictable.

"Have you made any progress with your mother's books?" Isaiah asked. She liked the excitement in his voice about her project. She wished she had made more progress but job hunting had distracted her.

"Why don't I come out and tell you about it while you work."

"Sure. I enjoy the company," Isaiah said.

She watched him take the tools he needed from the garage. He put out a knee pad before a stone path that had been laid years ago. The stones were worn and cracked. Denny had been saying for a long time that he wanted them pulled up and new stones set down. She guessed that was the task he had assigned Isaiah for the day.

"I have chosen a book for us to start working on. It is a pioneer story. A woman and her family are struggling to make a life in New Hampshire. Finally, the woman and her husband decide to move west and try their luck in Oregon."

"I like it," Isaiah said.

"The problem is that my mother only wrote the first bit. Once the characters get to their homestead there isn't much else in the manuscript. There were a few other manuscripts that were closer to complete but I was really drawn to these characters. It might even make a good series."

"I suppose you could have the first book be the adventures of getting to their homestead and then make sequels about life once they are there. Pioneer life was hard. I am sure that most any history book could give you ideas for the trials they would have faced. If I recall correctly cholera was a huge problem. Typhus too."

"Not to mention fires and flooding," Dawn agreed.

"Indians and cavalry," Isaiah added. Dawn laughed. It was fun using him as a sounding board for ideas. She could almost picture the series in her head. She was about to suggest that they make the fictional family Mormon and settling in Utah instead of protestant and heading to Oregon when Denny's car pulled into the driveway.

She watched Denny lift Julie's hands to his lips and give her knuckles a kiss. The look on his face told her they hadn't gotten the news they had hoped for.

Isaiah watched Julie hurry past him. Her eyes were red but her expression was stoic. The appointment obviously hadn't gone as planned. He knew all about getting news from doctors you didn't want to hear.

He felt a tingling in his throat. It was the same tingling he had felt time to time on his mission. It was a tingling he knew better than to ignore even though in this instance he really wanted to.

"I suppose it isn't any of my business but I thought perhaps I could start helping you get the nursery set up,"

Isaiah said once Denny had let Xander out of the car and transferred to his chair.

"A bit early for all that," Denny said. He looked exhausted.

"Sometimes being able to show our faith makes it easier for God to bless us."

Denny looked like he wanted to reply but he didn't. Isaiah shrugged. He had said it. Now, Denny could do with it whatever he needed to.

"Do you think it would upset Julie?" Denny asked. Isaiah turned to see that Dawn was only a yard away from them. She probably had heard everything he had said. He felt foolish but he pushed that thought away.

"I actually think it is a good idea. Then, when you finally are ready, it will be all set up," Dawn said. He was surprised and a bit relieved to have her take his side.

"I suppose so," Denny said though he looked unsure.

"And I know you and Julie have decided to adopt if the treatments don't work so no matter what the nursery won't go to waste," Dawn said.

"Let me ask Julie if she minds," Denny said after a long pause.

"I would wait until tomorrow," Isaiah said.

"I was planning on it," Denny said. He gave Isaiah a smile as he wheeled past him and up the ramp to the porch. Xander used a rope to pull open the door for him.

"I hope I didn't misspeak," Isaiah said to Dawn after the door was closed. The Spirit had moved him and he didn't regret his words however he wondered if it really had been right to say them at that moment. Was he still in tune with the Spirit as he had been on his mission?

"You didn't," Dawn assured him. "But I do think we should wait for another day to start the book. I think Julie needs some peace and quiet," Dawn said.

"Another time," Isaiah agreed. The stone path could wait another day.

"Are you doing okay?" Dawn asked Julie after Denny left to take Isaiah home. Talking to Isaiah had made her want to go through the pioneer manuscript again and start making notes but she needed to check on her friend first.

"I knew the chances of the treatment working the first time were small. I don't know why I feel so heartbroken about it," Julie said.

"Maybe because it is something you really want," Dawn said softly.

"Everything has been so hard. I just wanted this to be easy," Julie said. Dawn wished it was easier. Julie deserved to have something come easy to her.

"Think about how much more blessed you will feel because it wasn't easy," Dawn whispered. She put her arm around Julie and hugged her tightly.

"It isn't even just for me. I really want this for Denny. He doesn't talk about it much but I know that he thought that all his dreams were destroyed when that IED went off," Julie said. Dawn had not known Denny for as long as Julie had but she could imagine how devastating it would be for anyone to lose so much of their physical function.

"Denny knows how lucky he is. He knows this will take time. He has come a long way," Dawn said.

"I hate to admit it but I am glad Isaiah is here to help him. Denny hates asking my father for his for help but there are some things he just can't manage himself."

"Isaiah suggested starting to put together the nursery. It doesn't have to be anything big. Maybe just a coat of paint. It would give him and Denny something to work on." She hadn't planned on saying anything but the moment seemed right. She agreed with Isaiah that the nursery was something that Julie needed. If Dawn could convince her to accept the project for Denny she would be more able to accept it. Julie always was willing to help those she cared about.

"We are starting to run low on projects and Brother Campbell doesn't have any work for Isaiah. I know because I called him trying to find work for myself," Dawn added.

"Any luck with the job search?"

"None. I have applied a few places but nothing really exciting."

"If you could do anything and money wasn't an issue what would it be?" Julie asked.

"It sounds too crazy for words," Dawn admitted.

"Tell me anyways," Julie said.

"I want to finish my mom's books. Then, I want to write my own. Mom had so many good ideas but then she didn't take them the places I would have. Especially with heroines. I think it was because of the times she was raised in. All her characters are waiting to be rescued by heroes but most could rescue themselves if given half a chance and still end up married and living happily ever after. The thing is that I have no idea if there is money in writing and I need to be independent. I don't know if I will ever be as lucky as you and my mom with having a husband to support me. I want to make sure I can take care of myself but I think I want to be a writer deep in my heart." It sounded crazy even as she said it but it also was true. It was the first time she had voiced that wish aloud to anyone.

"Have you prayed about it?" Julie asked.

"No." Dawn admitted. Since the tragedy at work it had been hard to pray about something as trivial as job searches. All of her prayers had been for safety for her loved ones and comfort to families who had lost loved ones. She had started having nightmares about losing her mom. They had plagued her as a child but she had fewer as she became a teenager and as an adult they were very rare.

"I suppose all you can do right now it to try and pray about it. He will let you know one way or another what you are supposed to do," Julie said.

"I will," Dawn said.

She wished for the millionth time that her mother was alive and that she could call her. She had no idea what her mother would think of her dreams of being a writer or of her finishing her mother's stories. Her mother had never gone beyond writing for the pleasure of it. Would she think Dawn's dream a silly one?

Chapter 9

Dawn sat on the living room couch balancing her laptop on her thighs. Isaiah sat beside her with a green spiral notebook open on his lap. The neat loops of Dawn's mother's handwriting were written in faded ink that ranged in color from red to black. Isaiah could only guess that the writer had needed to start, stop, and restart her writing due to the demands of her family. Hadn't his mother always said how hard it was to get any task done when her children always seemed to need her for something? He had always needed her. He had needed her in California when he was sick. The nurse assured him that his parents had been notified but they had never called the hospital nor come to see him.

"I'm ready," Dawn said. She held her hands over the keys like he had been instructed in a school typing class a lifetime ago.

Isaiah read from the notebook. He made sure to say the words slowly so that Dawn's typing fingers could keep up.

"Greta couldn't remember the first time she had seen the man that she would grow up to marry. It might have been that he had grabbed the same jar of licorice at the candy store, played in the same fishing hole, or even shared the first day of school. All shc knew was by the time she started to notice him regularly around town he was as much a part of her surroundings as the yellow curtains that hung in her mother's parlor."

"Did Americans call them parlors?" Dawn asked lifting her fingers from the keys and tilting her face in his direction as if he might have the knowledge tucked somewhere in his brain. He wished he knew but he didn't.

"I have no idea. We can fact check it later."

"Okay. Go ahead."

"Greta married Thomas at eighteen and by the time she was thirty they had seven surviving children."

"I think I remember my mother saying she wished she could have had a large family. I wonder if she had lived if I would have other brothers and sisters," Dawn said softly.

"Feel like you are missing out a bit?" Isaiah asked.

"Maybe a little. Do you have any siblings?"

"Two sisters and a little brother," Isaiah said. Memories of them rushed into him making his heart ache. Eliza and Emma were identical twin girls who dressed alike and often acted like mirror images of each other. Emma had a small scar on her hand from a childish accident with their mother's sewing shears. It was the easiest way to tell the girls apart. Toby had been four when he left and just starting to really show his personality. He was the quietest and shyest of the family.

"Do you have contact with any of them?" Dawn asked.

"No. My sisters were preteens and my brother about to enter kindergarten when I left. I'm sure they didn't have the means to contact me, even if they wanted to."

"Maybe they will when they are older," Dawn said.

"Maybe," he agreed though he didn't really believe it. He had no idea what his parents had told his siblings but they probably hated him now too. He couldn't blame them. He had been the oldest child and always off with their father. Eliza had once teased him about being their father's favorite and he had explained it wasn't that he was the favorite but the oldest. He wondered now if the girls got more notice and attention from their father or if he had simply started to take more of an interest in Toby.

"Shall we continue?" Dawn asked. He nodded.

"Thomas worked hard every day and Greta ran a frugal household but they still struggled to support their family above the level of subsistence. One day while Thomas was at the post office he met a man who had come from Oregon."

"I think I want to change this part," Dawn said.

"How are you going to change it?" Isaiah asked.

"One day while Thomas was leaving the post office he ran into two young men who said they had a special message to deliver to Thomas from God," Dawn said as her fingers typed.

"A young boy named Joseph had been praying about which church to join. He had a vision where God and Jesus appeared and told him to join none of the faiths. Later, an angel named Moroni came to Joseph and directed him to a hillside where golden plates held a history of God's dealings with the people of the Americas. Joseph translated the words and this is the resulting book. They handed Thomas the Book of Mormon. Thomas and Greta read it and decided that they needed to join the saints in Utah," Isaiah said.

"You aren't half bad at this," Dawn said once she

finished typing.

The next scene in the book involved Greta and Thomas selling their home and loading up a wagon with their belongings.

"Can you stay for dinner?" Julie asked. Isaiah looked up. He hadn't noticed her enter the room.

"If it isn't too much trouble," Isaiah said.

"And assuming we aren't having any potato salad," Dawn added with a laugh. Isaiah laughed too at her good natured teasing.

He watched as she saved the document she had been typing and he glanced at the clock on the bottom of the screen. They had been working for three hours. He could barely believe it. It didn't seem possible that they had been there for so long.

"That was fun," Dawn said as she closed her computer and slipped it into a leather case.

"It was," Isaiah agreed.

"It really makes me feel connected to her. My mom I mean," Dawn said.

"I'm glad," Isaiah said. "Thanks for letting me be a part of this."

His heart ached for Dawn and the mother she had lost. Another part of his heart felt the smallest tinge of jealousy. Dawn's mother was dead and yet she could connect with her through some simple notebooks. His own mother was alive and still there was no way he could connect with her.

Dawn hurried to the silverware drawer and put out place settings on the table. Julie had cooked up a fine meal of steak gorgonzola which was one of her favorites. When Julie opened the oven the smell of garlic bread filled her nose and Dawn couldn't suppress a sigh.

"Seems like that project is going well," Denny said. He was at the table tossing a salad.

"It is. I would love to have it completed and a paperback copy to give to my dad when they come to my graduation."

"When do you graduate?" Isaiah asked.

"June." She had just gotten the dates and sent out announcements to her dad and Wilma to give to the Colorado family.

"Will your family be here for it?" Isaiah asked.

"They wouldn't miss it," Dawn said.

"Have you told your father about this project?" Isaiah asked.

"I mentioned it in passing," Dawn said. She had told Wilma what she was doing in more detail but she had only mentioned it to her father and Kyle. She didn't want the project to hurt them but she needed to do it for herself.

"I am sure they will be very proud of you," Julie said. Dawn hoped they would be.

Chapter 10

"It is looking good," Isaiah said as he stepped back to admire the drying paint. His whole body ached and his legs felt heavy but he had managed to completely paint the nursery in one day. The sun outside was setting so he guessed it had taken him seven hours. It was a large room but not so large that it would have taken anyone else more that a few.

"Do you think I can give Greta some sort of job?" Dawn asked. She was sitting in the center of the floor making notes in a spiral notebook with a red pen.

Listening to her talk about the book had made the hours seem to fly. They had finished Greta's story up until her family had arrived in the west. Now, Dawn was trying to figure out the rest of it.

"Perhaps making quilts?" Isaiah suggested.

"I was hoping to give her a skill fewer women had back then. I feel like most women in the nineteenth century could quilt."

"What about weaving?"

"I don't know."

"What does your mother have Greta doing?"

"She doesn't mention anything besides being a wife and mother."

"What is so wrong with that?" Isaiah asked.

"Nothing really. I just feel like giving her a job would add depth to her character."

"Or you could use her household responsibilities to

add to her character. Maybe she bakes a magnificent pie."

"Pie?"

"I could see pie making as a very important attribute in a woman," Isaiah said. "When I was growing up we had a wild raspberry bush in the back yard and I would go out and pick the berries for my mother. Have you ever picked raspberries?"

"Afraid not," Dawn admitted.

"They are thorny and your fingers get all scratched up. Then, the berry juice gets in the scratches and burns. It is quite a feat." He knew he was exaggerating the heroics of picking raspberries but her smile at his description made it worth it.

"And your mother made them into pie?"

"She did. All those scratches and burning fingers would be completely forgotten with just one bite of her pie."

He tried to push back the nostalgia but this time he couldn't. He could taste the raspberry pie on his tongue and his nose filled with the scent of his mother's kitchen.

His heart ached in his chest and he wondered if anyone picked the berries for his mother now. It had always been his job. His father would be too busy and his sisters had always been too prissy for the job. Their hands weren't calloused like his from outdoor work. They were tender and easily torn.

Maybe his brother had taken on the task since he was getting older or perhaps raspberry pies were now a thing of the past.

"Perhaps she can make pies for family and friends but

also sell them from time to time at the nearby military post," Dawn said. He watched her scribble a note at the top of the page.

"Your mother was a homemaker." He remembered that she had said so. "Maybe the reason so many of her characters aren't businesswomen is because she wasn't."

"But no one wants to read about characters who stay home, make elaborate meals, and raise babies," Dawn said.

"Who says so?"

"Everyone. We had a whole class about strong women in modern literature. Historically, so many women had to be passive. Look at how many women in history just let things happen to them. They let their father choose their husband and then they went meekly off to set up a household for the man their father said they should learn to love."

"And their real strength came exactly from that. Those women were put in less than ideal circumstances and still managed to thrive. They took care of the husband that their father had married them to and raised their children."

"I would think their lives would have been better if they had just refused to do what their father said."

"It probably would have been. But that doesn't mean it would have been right either."

"You went against your family to join the church. How can you say that doing what you are told is the better answer?"

"I did do what I was told. I just was following the orders of Heavenly Father and not my earthly father. It would have been so easy to say 'that isn't what I want to do. That looks too hard. I want to do it my way.' Don't think I never imagine the life I could have had. I would still be strong and healthy. I would still have my family around me. I wouldn't be here with no job."

"You regret your decision?"

"Never," he said. He hadn't even had to think about it. It had been a long hard road but there was nowhere he would have rather been than serving the Miller family.

"I suppose I can play with the story and see if leaving her as just a wife with a special ability to bake extraordinary pies is enough to keep things in motion," Dawn said quietly.

Isaiah felt his head beginning to ache. He wasn't sure if it was from the memories or paint fumes but he knew it was time to go back to Pete's house.

"I'm going to see if Denny is okay with this."

"It looks fine to me. I am sure it will look fine to him," Dawn said closing her notebook and getting to her feet.

"I'm sure that whatever job you give Greta she will excel at. Most people manage to acclimate. Greta can do the same."

He wished he could more easily acclimate. It was easy to say that a character in a story would eventually find their way no matter their circumstances. It was harder for him to see himself finally in the place God intended for him to be. He wasn't even sure what that place was now.

"Dawn, can you do something for me," Isaiah said. It was bold and he didn't know why but he felt compelled to say it anyways.

"What?"

"Pray for me." He needed to know he was in someone's prayers.

"Of course." Dawn reached out and squeezed his arm. It was a small gesture but she couldn't know what it meant to him.

Dawn watched from the window as Isaiah got into the car with Denny. She took a deep breath. She had liked hearing his stories about raspberries. It hadn't occurred to her until the very end that he was feeling homesick for a family he could never return to.

"I miss you mom," Dawn whispered. She had always believed that somewhere in Heaven her mother was watching over her and maybe even praying for her. She wondered if Isaiah's parents or the family who had converted him were praying for him.

He had been right to ask her to pray for him. Everyone needed someone to pray for their wellbeing. She had her family in Colorado. She also knew that Denny and Julie kept her in their prayers just as she prayed for them. It was something friends did. She and Isaiah had been spending so much time together. She could almost call him a friend.

Chapter 11

"Does it look ok?" Isaiah asked as he lined up the wallpaper border along the places he had marked with the leveler. He was on a ladder in the center of the wall and Dawn was on the floor.

Julie had chosen a dog border for the room. It was a yellow background with puppies playing in various poses. Isaiah was glad that they were able to find her design of choice pre-pasted.

"It looks fine," Dawn said. Isaiah firmly pushed the border against the painted wall, which he had sanded earlier, and smoothed it out.

"I wanted your opinion on another part of this book. I am thinking of adding a character to be Greta's best friend. Right now she mostly talks to her husband and children but I just think that it would be nice for her to have a friend to bounce ideas off of as well. My mom didn't have Greta leaving a best friend or making a best friend on the journey so I don't know if it would be out of character for her."

"Maybe her husband is her best friend."

"I don't think that was common back in the day."

"I'm not sure it is common now. That doesn't mean it isn't a good idea though," Isaiah said. Satisfied with the strip of border he slowly made his way down the ladder. His muscles were aching and his fatigue was starting to set in but he wanted to complete the border before Denny and Julie got home and there was only one more wall to do.

He leaned against the wall and lowered himself onto

the floor across from where Dawn was sitting with the capped end of her pen between her teeth as her head bent over the notebook in her lap. She wasn't chewing on it nervously as he had seen friends at school do. Instead, it was as if she was holding it like a retrieving dog did out of habit and the effects of nature. It didn't surprise him in the least that her mother had been a writer.

"Do you think Greta's best friend should be someone older or the same age? I like the idea of her learning from someone wiser and with more life experience but I think it is easier to relate to someone your own age and who is going through the same things you are."

"Pete and me are pretty close in age but I'm not sure that really helps us relate better," Isaiah said. Pete was a good friend but he had a very hard time understanding why Isaiah had trouble holding a job. Pete had never had a serious illness. He rather thought Denny was more able to relate to his current plight even though Denny was three or four years his senior.

He sighed and forced himself back up. There was only one more wall that needed a border. He could do one wall. He hated knowing how easy it had once been. When he was still at home in Missouri he wouldn't have even broken a sweat putting up borders in a single room.

He grabbed the last strip of border, moved the ladder, and began his ascent. His legs felt heavy and achy with each step he took but he pushed himself to the top.

"Maybe instead of a best friend I could give her a younger companion to mentor. Maybe a newly married woman in Relief Society. The woman could ask Greta to teach her about cooking and Greta could give her the secrets of a perfect pie. Maybe the younger girl is even a new mother and could use advice on how to take care of her baby. It has to be scary being a mother the first time around."

"Terrifying," a new voice said. Isaiah turned his head to the door to see Julie standing there. Tears were running down her cheeks. He had no idea what to say to her.

"You are going to have a baby?" Dawn asked. Julie had gone to the doctor to see if the last round of IVF had worked.

"More than one," Julie said.

"Twins!"

Julie shook her head and handed a black and white picture to Dawn. The paper had blotches of gray labeled A, B, and C.

"Triplets?"

"These two are identical," Julie said pointing to A and B.

"I can't imagine," Dawn said. She really couldn't imagine what it would be like to go from no children to three.

"Neither can Denny. He is still out in the car. I came in to share our news while he has a few moments to himself. It is all very tentative of course. The doctor warned us that it was entirely possible we could still have loses. It is still very early," Julie said. Dawn took Julie's trembling hands in hers.

"Congratulations," she said. She tried to think of what

a character would feel like in Julie's position. If she were writing about a woman who had just found out she was having three babies she would probably have made her overjoyed and equally terrified. She thought that was probably what Julie was feeling too from the shaking of her hands.

Julie's eyes ran around the room and stopped on Isaiah.

"The border is lovely," she whispered.

"Thanks," Isaiah said.

"It was a good idea. The sign of faith I mean."

"It is amazing that we just need faith the size of a mustard seed to move mountains but most of us can't manage even that," Isaiah said.

"I'm going to need a lot of faith now," Julie said quietly.

"And help," Dawn added.

"Definitely lots of that," Julie agreed.

"I'm here," Dawn said and she knew she would need to change her plans. Julie and Denny would need her help. Perhaps this was a sign from God that she wasn't meant to move out. She would stay with Denny and Julie as long as they needed. She wouldn't leave until Julie and Denny felt like they had the situation under control. If it had been her she was sure that she would have needed help until she shipped triplet children off to college. She might end up staying that long. She felt like she was stagnating. College would soon be over and there had been no offers for interviews at the places she had applied. The books her mother wrote were a fine pet project but she doubted they would turn her into a professional author. Even if she did become a professional author there would be plenty of time in her life to help Denny and Julie raise their babies. Those babies might be the only ones she ever had the chance to raise. Thirty seemed just around the corner and she hadn't even attempted to catch the attention of a man since the Valentine dance. She wasn't even sure she wanted to. Maybe she would never love anyone like Ben again.

Chapter 12

The knocking startled Dawn out of a sound sleep. She rolled over and looked at the clock on her cell phone. It was three AM. Who would be at their door at that hour?

She stood up and wandered into the hallway. Julie and Denny's door was still closed. She was surprised Xander hadn't woken them. He might be an amazing service dog but he certainly failed as a watchdog. She thought for a moment about waking them but Julie's body was resting for four people and Denny would be slow to transfer from the bed to the chair. In that time the knocker might wake the neighbors.

She hurried forward and glanced through the peep hole. In the dim light she almost didn't recognize Gwen Hawthorne. Gwen had gained weight since they last met and standing on the porch she was disheveled. Her face was red and her eyes swollen. Gwen's red hair was pulled back in a ponytail that was falling out at odd places around her face. She looked a mess.

Dawn threw open the door to let her in.

Gwen's car was out front. Had she driven all the way from California?

"I meant to get in hours ago but there was a semi that overturned and blocked up traffic for hours. I almost ran out of gas waiting," Gwen said.

She was trembling as she took a seat on the couch.

"Are you alright?"

"I didn't know where to go. I'm not ready to see my

parents yet. I thought Julie would let me spend the night at least. "

"I'm sure she won't mind. She is in bed now. Should I wake her?"

"It is better to let her sleep. My disasters are not worth risking my future nieces or nephews over," Gwen said.

"Let me get you a bottle of water," Dawn offered.

"Please, don't trouble yourself," Gwen said.

"It isn't any trouble. I am a good listener. And since you aren't my daughter or my sister I may be the best person for you to talk to. I'm not close enough to judge," Dawn said. It was mostly true. She had heard all about Gwen's less than stellar life choices from Julie but she had only met Gwen casually and so whatever trouble she was in would be far less upsetting to her.

She went to the refrigerator for the water and brought it back to Gwen. Then, she took a seat across from her in the living room.

Gwen opened the bottle and took a small sip before recapping it and leaning her head back against the chair.

"I'm getting a divorce," she whispered.

"I'm sorry," Dawn said.

"Ethan left me for another woman. I didn't make enough as a waitress to stay in California. We were already so in debt. I couldn't even live off the credit cards we had. I figured how much gas it would take me to get home. I packed up everything I really wanted and just started to drive. If I had gotten a flat tire or anything else like that I would have been stuck. Maybe forever," Gwen said. Dawn didn't point out that she was being overly dramatic.

Brother and Sister Hawthorne had been devastated when Gwen ran off without a word to California but they weren't the kind of parents who would refuse to help their child in need.

"I'm sorry," Dawn said again. She wasn't sure what else could be said.

"Her name was Chelsea."

"Who?"

"The woman Ethan fell in love with. She is a secretary at the construction company where he was working. I've met her a few times. She is everything I'm not. Blond. Thin. She is a really pretty girl. She is trying to be an actress. She goes to auditions after work and on her days off. I don't have any idea if she is any good, but Ethan must think she is. I was going to go to school but I just didn't think I could with my work hours. I was always getting called in to work extra and we needed the money. I thought a nice home would make Ethan happy. I really wanted to make him happy," Gwen said. She wasn't crying and Dawn wondered if she had cried herself out on the long drive. Had she stayed in motels along the way or slept in the back of her car at rest stops? Dawn was curious but didn't want to ask. It seemed rude.

"There isn't a spare bed but I can bring you a pillow and some blankets. Julie is usually up by seven," Dawn said.

"Thanks," Gwen said. She looked exhausted if not actually tired. It was likely that some sleep would do her as much good as anything.

Dawn went to the closet and pulled out a spare pillow

and a fleece throw.

Gwen had put her water bottle on a coaster and moved over to the couch. She tentatively fluffed the cushions.

"This will be fine," Gwen said taking the bedding from her.

"Try to get some sleep," Dawn said. She walked down the hall and listened but there was no sign that Denny, Julie, or Xander had been awoken by the noise so she made her way back to her room and climbed into bed.

She folded her arms and closed her eyes. She knew she should get out of bed and kneel but she was suddenly feeling too exhausted.

"Heavenly Father, thank you for all the blessing you have given me." It had been a while since she had truly felt grateful but it was nice to feel it. Seeing Gwen and hearing her story had put her own sorrows into perspective. She was fortunate and she needed to remember that and continue to push forward. It was easy to get discouraged but she couldn't let that stop her. Not now.

The sunlight streamed through the curtains and Isaiah rolled over to bury his face against his pillow. There had been a time when he was up well before the sun. In those days, when he was still in Missouri with his family, he had woken up to frying bacon and the smell of coffee. Now, he woke up to the smell of burning toast and the sound of Pete hurrying out of the door.

He wanted to stay in bed. His body felt heavy and his limbs ached but since his mind was awake he forced his body up as well.

After getting dressed and pouring a bowl of cereal he went to the computer and checked his email. There were no replies to the resumes or job applications he had sent out. They had mostly been long shots anyways. Logan Ohio didn't exactly have an abundance of jobs and most of the ones it had he couldn't physically do. Not fast enough to remain employed at any rate.

His inbox only had spam plus a single email from a family of converts he had known on his mission. They were letting him know that their first child had come into the world. Because of him, Sarah Bethany Michaels had been born in the covenant.

He finished his cereal and a tall glass of orange juice before glancing at the clock. The Miller's would be expecting him in another two hours. He showered, dressed, and then grabbed his scriptures for a hasty read.

He opened to Luke 14. It was a scripture he hadn't read for ages but it had been a favorite when he first joined the church. At the time verse 26 had been his favorite.

If any man come to me, and hate not his father, and mother, and wife, and children, and brethren, and sisters, yea, and his own life also, he cannot be my disciple.

The verse had made it easier to leave his parents' love for the gospel even though the Ten Commandments had instilled in him the laws of honoring his parents.

Now though, other verses meant more to him.

Verse 27 *And Whosoever doth not bear his cross and come after me, cannot be my disciple* spoke to him. He had become ill while serving his Father and bringing the gospel to people desperately in need. His illness was one of the crosses he had to bear. Most days, he accepted it but other days, like today, he had to fight away the anger.

He should have a job. Instead, he was doing odd jobs to make enough money to contribute to rent and utilities.

He should be working towards creating a family. He should be dating. Other men his age were getting engaged. A couple of his former companions were already married. How could he ask any girl to invest her time in him when he couldn't even keep a job? How could he hope to be a husband when his body felt so fatigued and sore that getting up each day was a challenge? He knew he couldn't.

It was his cross to bear.

He knelt down and folded his arms to pray.

"Father, bless my parents and siblings. Keep them safe. Soften their hearts so that they may be open to your truth and willing to hear the gospel.

Thank you for Pete and the Miller's for all the help they are giving me.

Please lead me to a job and help me understand what I am supposed to do. I know you have a purpose for me. Please, help me to find it."

It was a prayer he said almost every day. He knew that in His own time God would answer his prayers. He just had to be patient and that was no easy task.

Chapter 13

Dawn opened the door and walked in the house. Gwen was at the kitchen table chatting to Isaiah. She felt exhausted and contemplated going to her room to bed. Her shift had been a long one. There had been two code blues and one of them hadn't been revivable. The code that had died was only forty two. The family crying in the hallways had broken her heart. She wanted to curl under her covers and sleep but at just six o'clock in the evening it was too early to do that. She walked into the kitchen and pulled a bottle of apple juice from the refrigerator.

"I saw several fast food places on Main with help wanted signs," Isaiah said. Gwen nodded. Dawn glanced at the list in front of Gwen. It was places to apply for jobs. It was mostly retail and food places but for Gwen those jobs would be good starting points. Without a degree or much work experience her options were limited.

"I'll head over there and get some applications. My dad is firm that the only way I can come home is if I have a job. I have to start school or move out within six months," Gwen explained.

"Have you talked to the school counselors about your options yet? I am sure they will be glad to help," Isaiah said.

"Not yet."

"I can get you some phone numbers, if you like," Isaiah said.

"Thanks a bunch," Gwen said. She hopped off the

chair, grabbed her list, and made her way for the door.

"It's nice of you to try and help her," Dawn said. She hadn't been there when Julie had taken Gwen home to their parents' house but from what Julie had said it had been tense. Dawn had thought that Julie would let Gwen stay with them but no one had brought up that suggestion.

"It is always easier to help other people than help ourselves," Isaiah sighed.

"Have you ever thought that maybe that is the answer?" Dawn asked. She opened the cap and sipped her juice. It was cool and refreshing.

"What is the answer?"

"You could help other people for a living. Maybe be a social worker. Or a counselor." Dawn twisted the cap back on the juice.

"I don't think so," Isaiah said. Dawn shrugged.

"It was just a thought. There might even be something you could do online."

"Are you trying to get rid of me?" he asked. She could tell from his smile that he was teasing.

"Just trying to help you. I appreciate all the work you have put into helping me with my mother's manuscripts. Did I tell you I have the first one, Greta's Song, almost ready to self publish?"

"Congrats. I hope people love it."

"I hope so too. I think I am going to throw a book launch party once my parents come in for graduation. Do you want to come?" Dawn asked. She hadn't actually been planning any such thing but once the idea came into her head it seemed brilliant. It was something her mother would have loved.

"Sure," Isaiah said. "Do you need any help planning it?"

"That would be great," Dawn said. "Have you ever planned a party before?"

"Never. But I am a pretty fast learner. A few internet searches and we should have a pretty basic idea," Isaiah said.

Dawn's heart fluttered with excitement. The book had started as her mother's but she had added to it significantly. It was something they would forever share.

In just one month she would graduate from college and publish her first book.

Isaiah walked into the nursery where Julie was standing. He turned around to go so as not to disturb her but she motioned for him to come in.

"I'm trying to decide whether to buy three cribs now," she whispered. "I just passed twelve weeks and all three babies still have heartbeats."

"What does Denny say?"

"We have only discussed it briefly. I think he is still in shock. Either that or he is terrified. Not having a child would be easier than losing three or even one of them now."

He looked Julie over and noticed for the first time that even though her clothes hung loosely her belly had begun to show the signs of life inside of her. It might have been easier during the first few weeks to put the idea of new life out of mind. Now though, Denny would be able to see it.

Isaiah didn't even want to try to imagine how pained his friend would be if the babies didn't make it.

"If you buy the cribs I will put them up for you," Isaiah offered.

"And take them down if needed?" Julie asked.

"Of course," Isaiah said. Julie gave a slight nod.

"Did you want me to finish putting up the pictures?" Isaiah asked. Julie had bought several pictures that matched the border and shown him where to hang them. It was obvious that they were running out of work for him to do.

Maybe Dawn wasn't so far off. He needed to find work. It probably took lots of schooling to become a counselor or a life coach but maybe he could do some kind of inexpensive mentoring for people hard on their luck. Maybe people would pay him just to listen to their problems and help them solve those problems that were solvable. It could probably be done over the internet. He would need to do some research. Maybe no one would even be interested but even if he could only help a few people at first it might give him enough money to pay his bills. With some kind of steady income he could go to college. Maybe he could even live in the dorms so that Pete could have his space back again.

Then, maybe, just maybe, he could get his life somewhat back on track.

Chapter 14

Dawn rushed forward to hug her father, Wilma, and Kyle. She had been waiting for their plane to arrive for ages. It had been delayed first ten minutes and then half an hour. She didn't think she could bear to wait any longer.

"I'll go get our bags," Kyle offered. Dawn couldn't believe how much older he looked since last time she had seen him. He had broadened in the shoulders and it felt as if he had added an inch to his height. She guessed he must be almost six foot tall now. When she had last seen him his dark blond hair had been shaggy but now it was clean cut.

"And I will go see about the rental car," Wilma said. Dawn noticed that she had recently dyed her hair. It was a natural looking red and close to the color she had been born with though gray had begun to show recently.

"We are all so excited for you, Pumpkin," Dawn's dad said. She noticed his hairline had receded further leaving him halfway bald. Despite the continued hair loss he looked like he was feeling better. After his heart attack he had looked ill for a time but it seemed returning home to Colorado had been enough to reinvigorate him.

"I am excited too," Dawn said.

"I know your mom would be proud," her dad said. She noticed that he had lost weight since the move. Hopefully that meant he was following the doctor's orders of better eating habits and more exercise.

"Yeah, I think she would be too."

"Have you figured out what you are going to do after

graduation? Any of those job applications bear fruit?"

"I haven't heard anything yet. I don't want to be in too big of a hurry to leave. Julie and Denny are going to need help once their babies arrive."

"It is good of you to want to help them but just make sure you don't put your own life on hold for them either. You make sure you are listening to the Spirit and not just making decisions based on concern for your friends."

"I guess it will just be wait and see for a while," Dawn said. She felt peaceful about her choice to remain. It wasn't the time or place for her to move on. She had wanted to leave her job at the hospital but even that seemed less urgent these days. She had been concentrating so hard on finishing the first Greta book that her days at work flew by as she brainstormed.

"We got a suite at the hotel so if you want to stay the night you can. I thought we could catch up. Maybe have pizza and a movie like we did when you were little."

"That would be fun," Dawn agreed. It made her a bit sad that her family would only be there for the weekend. Tomorrow she would graduate and then she would have her book launch party. Her family would join her at church on Sunday and then they would get back on a plane Monday morning so that her parents could work on Tuesday.

Isaiah typed "mentor" into the web browser and put on a filter for videos. He wasn't surprised by how many results he got back.

Dawn had been right that he wanted to help people.

He loved serving others with his father when he was a child and on his mission he had equally loved it. So many people in the world were struggling. If he could be a light to any of them he would.

He pulled up the first video and watched as a Hispanic gentleman talked about the need for education and frequent reading. Then, a southern lady who seemed to have too much caffeine in her system talked about using the Bible to understand your purpose and to set God oriented goals.

Several people of various genders and ethnicities had videos about starting businesses, investing, and goal setting.

His eyes burned with exhaustion as he closed the last listed video on the third page of results.

"Is that webcam you have any good?" Isaiah asked as Pete came through the door with Chinese take out. Isaiah took the white box offered to him and opened it up. The smell of lemon chicken over fried rice teased his nose but his mind was running at full speed.

"It isn't studio worthy but it is passable. What do you need it for?"

"I am thinking about putting up some videos online. There are several websites that pay you when people watch your videos. I was thinking I could start there. Nothing big. Mostly inspirational type stuff for Mormons."

"I guess that wouldn't hurt. Any way to spread the gospel and help other members has to be positive," Pete agreed.

"I might even take a cue from Dawn and see if I can

write a book or two. I would love to share my conversion story with others."

"Isn't there liability and legal issues with all that?"

"I have no idea. I am still just learning everything," Isaiah admitted.

He turned back to the computer feeling a wave of energy flow through him.

He was going to use the talents he had been given and help serve other people. Maybe he would make money doing it. Maybe he wouldn't. What mattered was that he had a plan and a purpose he could pursue. He looked at the clock. It was just shy of seven. He could work for three more hours before he needed to turn in. Dawn's book launch party was the next day and he had promised to help. He wasn't going to let her down. She had helped him find his purpose and there was no way he was going to miss helping her celebrate hers.

Chapter 15

Dawn felt a dozen different emotions as she accepted her bachelor's degree. Partially, she felt relief that all of her schooling was completed. She also felt trepidation about her future. What would life hold? Would she finish completing her mother's books or would she find a job? She hadn't felt so unsure of life since Ben had left.

"Can we take you out to dinner to celebrate?" her father asked as she returned to them after the ceremony was completed.

"Actually, we are having a party. A friend is setting it up right now," Dawn said. Her stomach felt nervous with anticipation as they walked to the car her dad had rented.

"Just give us directions," Wilma said as she climbed into the passenger seat. Dawn took her place in a captain's chair behind her dad. Kyle was across from her.

She directed them to the hall she had rented for two hours.

She took a deep breath as they pulled in. A sign out front read *Congratulations Dawn*. Denny's car was in the parking lot as well as his parent's, the Hawthorne's, and several other friends.

Dawn led them inside. Immediately, she was overwhelmed by the setup. Isaiah and her friends had gone out of their way for her party. A table against the back wall held sandwiches and finger foods. In the center of the room were six round tables with folding chairs.

At the entrance of the room was a small table which

held twenty copies of her book.

She had spent the week after finals finishing the formatting and creating a cover. Isaiah had helped her with that part of things and she had been pleased with the results. The cover showed a pioneer woman in front of a covered wagon. It might not have been terribly original but that didn't stop her from taking pride in it.

"Is this what you made from that box of notebooks?" her father asked approaching the table.

"The first of many I hope," Dawn said.

"They are lovely," Wilma said. She picked up one of the books and ran her fingers over the cover.

"Nice work," Kyle said.

"You will have to send me a copy. I want to read it," Wilma said.

"Of course," Dawn agreed. She motioned for Isaiah, who had been standing at the front of the room to join them.

"And who is this?" Wilma asked giving Dawn a sly smile.

"This is my friend, Isaiah," Dawn said emphasizing the word 'friend'. "He helped me with this. I couldn't have done it without him," Dawn said and she really did mean it. She couldn't imagine having undertaken such a project all by herself.

"I just read the notebooks so she could type them," Isaiah said.

"And he let me use him as a sounding board for my ideas," Dawn added.

"Well, that too," Isaiah agreed with a shrug.

"And he set this party up for me," Dawn said.

"She told me what she wanted," Isaiah said.

"I had assumed it was your roommate, Julie, who had set it all up," Wilma said.

"I am sure she would have but we all want her to take it easy," Dawn said. Julie had been acting so tired recently that Dawn couldn't imagine her doing anything. Even if she had been able and willing Dawn doubted Denny would have let her and she couldn't blame him.

"Oh yes. I almost forgot about the babies," Wilma said.

"Your roommate is having twins?" her father asked.

"Triplets," Dawn corrected. She was pretty sure she had told her father all about it but it was probably something she mentioned in passing to him and spoke more in depth to Wilma about.

"Such a blessing," Wilma said. Dawn tried to ignore the hurt in her eyes. She wondered if her step-mother had ever wished for her own children. Dawn knew she and Kyle had been a handful but it had never occurred to her that her step-mother might have wished for a larger family than she had gotten.

"We are so proud of you," Sister Miller said coming up behind her. She had one of the books in hand and clearly had been reading the first chapter. "This is good work. I think you will end up a very famous author if you keep this up."

"It was my mother's idea. I just built on it," Dawn said.

"I am sure your mother would be very proud," Wilma

said squeezing her shoulder.

"I think I will make a writing desk for your room. I've been meaning to try something challenging," her father said.

"I won't be coming to Colorado. At least not for a while. Julie needs me to help once the babies come," Dawn said.

"And we wouldn't want to pull her away from such a nice young man," Wilma said motioning to Isaiah who blushed.

"I think we should eat now," Dawn said because it seemed like the only thing to say to break the awkwardness of the moment.

Isaiah left Dawn to her family and went to the table and grabbed a plate. Hesitantly, he put two finger sandwiches, cheese cubes, fruit, and cookies on the plate before sitting down at the table where Denny, Julie, the Millers, and Hawthornes were.

He had never met Julie's parents or her younger sister Stacy.

"We might just have to have you plan Julie's baby shower," Sister Hawthorne teased.

"Thank you kindly but I don't plan to hand in my hammer for a party planning venue just yet."

"Oh yes, I forgot you were doing handyman work for my daughter," she said.

"Do you suppose we could hire you for a project? See, we raise guinea pigs and we want to redo the cages that we currently have. There just isn't room for all of them. I've got a basic plan laid out for stackable cages but I could really use an extra hand," Brother Hawthorne said.

"I'd be glad to," Isaiah said. "I'm just a bit slow at the work."

"No problem. Slow is better than not at all. Three daughters and not one likes tools," Brother Miller said.

Isaiah laughed politely and tried to push away the sadness that threatened to envelope him. Had his brother taken over helping their father with repairs or did the people he had grown up serving simply go without now that he wasn't there for them?

Chapter 16

"Do you think I should wait until I know what they are?" Julie asked.

"These would be fine for either boys or girls," Dawn said lifting up a green onesie. They had gone to the mall for maternity clothes. Julie's wardrobe was beginning to be too snug around her middle. Naturally, they hadn't been able to avoid the draw of one of the stores specializing in baby items. All of the baby items made Dawn wonder if she would ever have a child of her own to shop for. Shopping for Julie's babies was fun but it also brought out a maternal longing in her heart. Greta was a maternal character and the more she had written her the more she had realized her own mother's deep love for her and Kyle.

"I'm past the first trimester now so I suppose buying a few of these wouldn't hurt," Julie said. She picked up three white, three yellow, and three green onesies.

"Did the doctor say when you would find out what you are having?" Dawn asked.

"In another four weeks I have an ultrasound scheduled. They will try to take a peek then. I honestly don't care as long as they are healthy," Julie said. It might have been clichéd if she wasn't carrying triplets but Dawn thought Julie probably did feel exactly that way. She had done some internet searches about triplet pregnancy and the dangers for both mother and babies were more than she had expected.

"I will carry that," Dawn said taking the bag from the

store clerk.

"I could have managed," Julie said.

"I know. But that isn't the point," Dawn smiled.

Julie stepped out of the store and turned right around the corner. Dawn was behind her when she stopped abruptly and nearly ran into her.

It took a moment for Dawn to see what Julie was looking at.

Gwen was seated on one of the benches near the central fountain. She wasn't alone. She was actually deeply involved in a kiss with a guy whose face Dawn couldn't make out.

All she could really see of the guy was his dyed blue hair and a snake tattoo slithering down his neck.

Dawn reached out and took Julie's hand pulling her away from the scene before them and led her into a nearby clothing store.

"I'm pretty sure they have a maternity section here," Dawn whispered.

"I'm not sure I feel like shopping anymore," Julie said.

"I know but you have to. Your clothes barely fit and as those babies keep growing things will only get worse," Dawn said. Julie nodded but Dawn wasn't sure whether she had even heard her.

"She just can't seem to stay out of trouble," Julie whispered.

"Maybe things aren't as bad as they look," Dawn said though she doubted her own words.

"I had hoped that mother's strict rules would help her get her life back on track. It doesn't seem like that is working. She shouldn't be at the mall kissing any boy. Especially not one like that."

"There isn't anything you can do for her," Dawn said.

"That doesn't make me want to help her any less. I pray for her every night but God can only help her as much as she is willing to help herself. I don't want to see her married to another man like Ethan."

"Maybe things aren't that serious."

"That would be even worse."

Dawn sighed. She understood exactly what Julie meant. She looked around for the sign indicating the maternity section and she pointed to it. Julie reluctantly followed.

The maternity section was small and the selection was sparse but Julie found three pairs of elastic waist pants that fit her as well as four shirts with room in the belly area. One looked like a lit hotel sign and read "no vacancy' which made Julie laugh. Once she had paid for the purchases and gone back to the mall concourse Gwen and the man with the tattoo were nowhere to be seen.

"If you don't have any more work for me after this I understand. I just started working online and I think it will bring in enough to meet my needs," Isaiah said. He also had spent the last weekend helping Julie's father build cages for the guinea pigs. They had paid him more generously than he had expected.

Denny had been very quiet as they put together the first of the three matching white cribs.

"What are you doing?" Denny asked.

"I'm becoming a mentor."

"Like a counselor?"

"Not exactly. I will be making inspirational videos and posting them online."

"That is a real business?" Denny asked. Isaiah understood why he was doubtful.

"There are plenty of mentors and life coaches online already. I couldn't find any specifically catering to Mormons though. We have our own unique challenges."

"That is true," Denny agreed.

"I found several life coaches who were Evangelical Christians. They were creating podcasts and videos to help uplift people of their faith."

"Don't you think you are rushing into it? It seems very sudden."

"I wasn't doing anything else. Maybe this will pay the bills and maybe it won't but it is certainly better than nothing. I kept praying for an answer about what I am supposed to do. For now, this feels like the right thing," Isaiah said. The idea seemed just as crazy to him but something about it also felt right. It wasn't the first leap of faith he had taken. It would be a way for him to help others and work even with the limitations on his body. Maybe he would make money. Maybe he wouldn't. Maybe God would open some other door for him. All he knew was he had to try.

"I suppose if you are giving out advice you could start with me."

"I don't see how I can be of much help to you," Isaiah

said. If there was ever someone Isaiah had met who seemed to have things together it was Denny.

"I've been offered the calling of Bishop. I haven't accepted it yet."

Isaiah let the words sink in for several moments before he replied.

"What does Julie think?" Isaiah asked.

"She has the faith to believe that if God calls me to it he will give me the tools to succeed. I'm not so sure."

"Why?" Isaiah asked.

"It couldn't be a worse time. I'm just finishing up school. It will take so much of my time. Then of course there is Julie and the babies. Our lives are so up in the air. I don't feel like I have the strength to take care of everything I already have in my life."

"You don't need strength. You just need faith. Weakness is a gift from God," Isaiah said.

"It doesn't feel like much of a gift," Denny said.

"Do you have your scriptures? I just read about this last night," Isaiah said.

"On the table in the living room," Denny said.

Isaiah went to the living room and picked up the quad. He came back to the room and sat down on the floor beside Denny's chair. He turned to The Book of Ether Chapter twelve. He ran his finger down the page until he found verse 27.

"And if men come unto me I will show unto them their weakness. I give unto men weakness that they may be humble; and my grace is sufficient for all men that humble themselves before me; for if they humble themselves before

me, and have faith in me, then will I make weak things become strong unto them.

If you weren't worried about whether you were ready to serve as Bishop you probably wouldn't really be ready to do it. That is what the scriptures say. If you have faith that you are being called of God then He will help you overcome that weakness."

"It sounds like something Julie would tell me. I haven't really talked to her in depth about it all. I think I am worried about upsetting her. I want to be strong for her because I can only imagine all that she is going through right now. When the doctor said she was pregnant with three babies I didn't even know what to think. In many ways it is easier for me. I get to go to work and come home and parent but she will be home with three babies all day by herself.

The doctor said she might even lose one or more of them. It is pretty common, apparently. I've seen the pictures on the ultrasound but I know I am not connected to them like she is. They aren't really real to me yet. Even the ultrasound pictures just look like dark circles to me. I think she can really see the babies in those pictures. I can't. I just want to make sure she can get through this but I have no idea how to help her either."

"Julie is one of the strongest women I know," Isaiah said. It was true. His mother had been a strong woman but she couldn't compare to either Julie or Dawn. Maybe if she could have she wouldn't have submitted to his father and left him exiled because he had found the gospel.

"I knew that having babies would be hard. I just didn't

think it would be this hard," Denny said.

Isaiah couldn't imagine. He hadn't stopped and thought about having children and raising a family. When he had first converted his whole focus had been on his mission. After getting sick he had only thought about finding a way to work again. Now that life was coming together for him he realized that family was something he should be thinking of. It was the first commandment God had given to mankind. It was a man's most sacred responsibility. It had seemed impossible just months before that he would ever be able to contemplate having a family. It didn't seem so impossible now. Not when he was sitting beside Denny who was about to be the father of triplets even though he was wheelchair bound.

Chapter 17

Dawn was surprised to hear the knock at the door. Denny and Julie were at a doctor appointment to check on the health of Julie and the triplets. A glance at the clock told her who was at the door but the fact that Isaiah had chosen to come over surprised her and made her giddy.

"I wasn't sure you would come," Dawn said as she opened the door to let Isaiah enter.

"Because there is no more odd jobs from Denny?" Isaiah asked.

"He said you started your own business. Something like life coaching."

"Something like it," Isaiah agreed.

"How is that going?"

"Really well. I am enjoying helping people. I figured that even though Denny didn't need me you still probably wanted help with your books. Thought I could hang out and you could tell me what the latest and greatest happening with Greta is," Isaiah said. Dawn had barely touched the manuscript in days. Wilma had called to say that she loved the first book and several friends who had been at the launch party had also complimented her. In many ways it was nice but it also suddenly was terrifying. Her mother had started the first book. Dawn had only finished it. She had attempted to start the second book but she thought she might be stuck. She didn't know what she wanted to write next and it made her think of even giving the whole writing dream up.

"I had Greta's husband injured in a cattle stampede but now I am not sure what should happen."

"Any permanent injuries to him?"

"No. He just was down a few days and she had to do all his chores for him. Put her pie business on hold."

"Maybe you could introduce a new character. Someone to be a new friend to her husband."

"I suppose I could do that," Dawn said but she wasn't sure if that was really where she saw the book going. Greta had plenty of friends. It seemed like adding more might just be fluffing the book. She wanted the second book to be her masterpiece but she had never felt so incapable in her life.

"If you don't want people you can always have drought or fires for tension."

"You don't think that it would be too much?" Dawn asked. She didn't want to give the story a feeling of unreality.

"I think that life is hard," Isaiah said. Dawn nodded slowly. Then, she felt the spark of an idea.

"Suppose Greta had been so scatterbrained from trying to do her husband's work that she left something near the fire. Suddenly, all they had went up in flames. Greta blames herself and feels as if coming out was a mistake but her husband assures her that they will rebuild and it will be even better than what they already created," Dawn said.

"I like that idea. It makes sense with her husband's injury but also adds new drama and challenges," Isaiah said.

"Let me get my laptop," Dawn said. She hurried into

her room feeling the warmth of excitement flowing through her. No one supported her like Isaiah did and no one else inspired her muse. Julie read over what she wrote from time to time but Julie didn't have the same sense of storytelling that Isaiah seemed to. She could say what she liked and didn't but she wasn't nearly as good as Isaiah for bouncing ideas off of.

With her laptop under her arm Dawn rounded the corner into the living room and stopped in her tracks. Isaiah was holding Gwen against his chest and stroking her hair. An unpleasant feeling flooded through Dawn. She didn't have time to name the feeling before she heard the sobs coming from Gwen.

"Is it Julie?" Dawn asked. Isaiah shook his head.

Gwen pulled away from Isaiah and threw her arms around Dawn.

"I'm sorry. He said Julie wasn't home. I thought I could wait to fall apart until she was." Gwen's body shook as she cried against her.

"It is okay. What happened?" Dawn asked feeling her sleeve growing wet with tears.

"I just got back from the doctor and I am sick," Gwen said.

"Sick? How are you sick?" The first thought that sprang to Dawn's mind was cancer.

"I have syphilis."

"Oh my," Dawn said. Working in healthcare she knew a little about syphilis including how one came to have such an illness.

"I was seeing this new guy and he gave it to me,"

Gwen cried.

"Did the doctor give you medicine? I do believe it is very treatable," Dawn said. In the old days she knew people had gone mad and even died from the disease but as far as she knew it was now almost never deadly if caught in time.

"Of course he did. That isn't the point though. I didn't think something like that really happened to people like me. I mean, I wasn't... you know. I was only with one person."

"Perhaps you should be glad it was something as treatable as syphilis," Dawn said though she knew it was a harsh thing to say. Still, if Gwen had put herself in a situation where she could contract syphilis she must also be in a situation where she could contract more deadly diseases such as hepatitis and HIV.

"My life is such a mess," Gwen cried. "This wasn't at all how I thought things would be, you know."

"Life often takes unexpected turns," Isaiah said.

"I was supposed to be married and making a life with Ethan. I was supposed to be far away from Ohio," Gwen said.

Dawn wanted to point out that no ones life seemed to go as planned. She should be a married woman now but Ben had left her and his faith. If he hadn't, she wouldn't be living with Denny and Julie. She would be making her own home and maybe by now she would even have a child or two. She could understand the desire to wallow in self pity but it did no good.

"I was supposed to serve a full mission but that didn't happen either," Isaiah said. "There are two types of challenges we face as people. Those brought on ourselves by our sins and those brought by God to strengthen us or lead us to the path He wants for us."

"So you are saying God gave me syphilis to punish me?" Gwen asked looking indignant.

"I think it is more likely that he allowed you to get it to warn you away from the life you were leading. Maybe to prevent worse things from happening to you," Isaiah said softly. The words hadn't sounded so harsh in his head.

"That is ridiculous," Gwen said. Her face flushed and she balled her hands into fists. He wondered if she would take a swipe at him.

"If there is a God then why do bad things happen to people who are both good and bad? Why give me a disease to help me correct my life but not give it to someone else who is doing way worse stuff than me? I was with one guy. What about all the women who are promiscuous? What about the women exchanging their bodies for drugs? Does God make them sick to save them? It must not work very well because it seems like most of them just go right back to what they were doing." Gwen's voice was almost shouting. He was glad Denny and Julie weren't there to witness the exchange. He certainly hadn't meant to hurt Gwen with his words. He was only trying to help.

"I didn't say everyone listens. Gwen, you were born in the covenant which gives you special protections. Your parents taught you the gospel. Satan works harder on those who know God's truth. Do you think most of the people you mentioned who are promiscuous or using drugs know the power of God's love? They don't know the things you do and God will judge them accordingly."

"You are judging me!" Gwen's voice was high and hurt. He realized he should have stopped speaking but it was as if he couldn't.

"It isn't my place to judge anyone. I am just trying to help."

Gwen released a series of expletives at him before she turned around and stomped towards the door. He begged Dawn with his eyes to stop Gwen. He hadn't meant to upset her. He just wanted her to see that if she let it, her illness could be a blessing. It could help her turn her life around. If she didn't, next time things could be worse.

Of course, if all he had said was true than how could he justify himself getting sick when he was on the righteous path?

God hadn't warned him about the potato salad. It hadn't been his own wickedness or ignoring the Spirit that had made him sick. Though he had continued to pray about it he still didn't feel as if he had any idea why God had let him get sick.

He could have served others better if his body was still strong. He could have continued to convert people on his mission. He wasn't any better off being almost homeless in Ohio because he had gotten sick.

Perhaps before he threw proverbial stones at Gwen he needed to figure out why God had allowed him to get sick. What was he missing? He needed to start praying for understanding because he still felt like there was a piece of the puzzle of his life that didn't fit.

"I was a real jerk just now to her. Wasn't I?" Isaiah asked.

"I know you were just trying to help," Dawn said. He hoped she did know that. All he ever wanted to do was help people. If Gwen could only open up her eyes and see her own worth she would stop sinning. How could any daughter of God put themselves in the position she was in? It was easy enough for people who didn't know their place in God's plan but how could anyone who knew that they were a literal child of God and able to attain Godhood through obedience live the life she was living? He had wanted to spread that message to the world through his mission. He had wanted to take it to every poor suffering soul in the world and let them know their true value. Yet, he couldn't even convince someone who had been raised in the faith to see God's loving hand in their suffering and sorrows.

"I need to go," Isaiah said.

He rushed forward to the door and threw it open. Gwen was already gone but he hadn't planned to chase her. He needed time. He needed space. He started to walk. He wanted to walk and pray until he was exhausted. Then, he would call Pete and get a ride. For the moment he needed solitude and silence.

Dawn wanted to chase after him but she held herself back. He needed to face his demons alone and she needed to let him. She wasn't truly sure what had set him off but she knew that whatever it was went beyond her ability to assist him.

She grabbed her phone and sent a text to Julie to fill her in on the situation both with Gwen and Isaiah. Then, she took her laptop back to her room. She didn't feel much like writing now. Greta and her problems could wait another day.

Chapter 18

"I don't think you have eaten a meal this week," Pete said.

"I have. You just haven't seen me," Isaiah said. He opened his online bank account and reviewed his balance. He was far from wealthy but there was more money in his account than there had been in months. He double checked his check book including the amounts he had paid on his tithing. The numbers were right even though it was more than he thought he should have. Julie's father had paid him for his work on the guinea pig cages and Denny had paid him for his handyman work and there had been some views of his online videos. He hadn't thought it had all added up to quite so much.

He looked and made sure he had paid Pete his portion of rent and utilities but try as he might there was no mistake he could see.

The amount in the account was enough to rent an apartment. It would cover at least the deposit, first month, and last month of rent with money to spare. It might even be enough for a clunker of a car. He would have been better off saving the money and he knew that but he couldn't. Not when he felt so strongly that he needed to get on his own feet.

"You want a sandwich?" Pete asked walking into the kitchen.

"Not right now."

"Fasting again?"

"I need answers," Isaiah said.

"Just make sure you don't overdo it, okay. God doesn't want you to get sick."

"I feel great," Isaiah said. It was true. He did. He felt good enough for some sunshine and fresh air.

Dawn heard the knock on the door but she didn't move to answer it. She was in the middle of editing her book. Julie was out in the kitchen and close enough to answer the door.

She was surprised to hear her name called. She closed her laptop and walked into the living room. Isaiah was standing there in overalls and she couldn't help laughing at the sight of him.

"What are you doing?" she asked.

"I came to see if you wanted to go berry picking. Pete let me borrow his car for the day and I thought that with such nice weather it was time to give you some berry picking and pie baking experience so that you can write what you know. Isn't that what writers are always being told?" Isaiah asked.

"Are you serious?" Dawn asked.

"I sure am," Isaiah assured her. She laughed. It was crazy but maybe the experience really would help her writing. At the very least, it would be fun.

"Give me ten minutes to change," Dawn said. She hurried to her room and changed into a worn pair of jeans and an old faded t-shirt. Both jeans and shirt had paint stains from service projects of the past. They would be perfect for a day berry picking.

Isaiah had remembered a house he had biked by in Logan having several raspberry plants. He had decided to be bold and knock on the owner's door to ask if he could come by later with a friend to pick berries. The owner was an elderly man who had told him to help himself. Isaiah had insisted the man take ten dollars for the privilege though the man was clear that he would let them pick for free.

He pulled into the drive way and three cats rushed forward to greet them. Dawn got out of the car and gave them each a good scratch before Isaiah handed her a pail and led her back to the berry bushes.

"Mind your fingers," he warned. The scratches from the thorns were not too painful but if berry juice got into the scratches it stung.

"They smell so nice," Dawn said.

"Yes, they do," Isaiah agreed. The berry bush smelled of his childhood summers.

"I can imagine Greta and her children doing this," Dawn said.

"And maybe eating a few as well," he said taking a berry and popping it into his mouth. They were at the peak of ripeness and more sweet than sour.

Dawn tried one too.

"These are really good. They taste different than the ones at the store," Dawn said.

"Fresh fruits and vegetables always do," Isaiah said.

"Could you imagine how much work it would be for Greta to pick all the berries she would need to bake pies for selling? Picking a few for the family would not be bad but they would have needed baskets and baskets if she was selling pie," Dawn said.

"Pioneers worked hard," Isaiah said.

The cats wandered over and Isaiah threw a raspberry to one who batted it like a marble.

"What are we going to do with all these berries? My pail is half full," Dawn said.

"I thought we would bake a pie," Isaiah said.

"I have never baked a pie," Dawn confessed.

"I can teach you," Isaiah said.

He had never actually made one by himself but he had watched his mother bake them. Plus, he had looked up pie making videos online the night before. He had taken down notes as well as made a grocery list.

"I wish I had brought a notebook with me. I really want to capture the essence of this experience," Dawn said.

Isaiah reached in his front pocket and pulled out a small memo pad.

He continued to pick berries as the cats batted berries at his feet and Dawn took notes.

It was nearing dinner time when both pails were full.

"Ready?" Isaiah asked. Dawn was smiling so brightly. Her joy filled his heart.

"I don't want it to end," Dawn admitted.

"But the best part is yet to come. You haven't even eaten the pie yet," he said and they both laughed.

Isaiah left one pail of berries on the property owner's doorstep and he poured the rest into a plastic storage container.

They stopped along the way to get the supplies that they would need for baking the pie and then they returned to Dawn's house. A note on the refrigerator indicated that Julie and Denny had gone to the Hawthorne's house for dinner.

"At least that means we won't be in anyone's way," Dawn said.

Dawn had wanted to grab pre-made pastry crust but Isaiah had insisted they do if from scratch.

He took out a mixing bowl and Dawn measured out the flour, butter, salt, and water.

She mixed the ingredients together while he floured a section of the counter for them to work the dough.

He looked over at Dawn as she mixed. The whole scene with them together in the kitchen felt so domestic. He felt for the first time in a long time as if he was finally home.

Dawn was going to be a very good wife for some man.

He felt the tug of the Spirit like he had not felt since the confirmation that the Book of Mormon was true. Dawn was supposed to be his wife. He knew it as surely as he knew that the church was true.

He wanted to protest. He just now was finding his financial footing. He did not have a secure job. Dawn needed a man with a secure job so she could be a writer. She needed a man who could take care of her. He could barely take care of himself.

Dawn was his friend. He didn't know if she felt anything for him beyond friendship. He had never really dated any woman. He didn't know what he should do.

"I need to go," Isaiah said.

"Right now?" Dawn asked.

"I'm not feeling so well," Isaiah said. It wasn't even a lie. He felt a weight on his chest. He didn't know if it was from the day of physical exertion or from the revelation that he had found the woman who was supposed to be his eternal companion and he was not ready.

"I hope you feel better," Dawn called as he rushed towards the door.

Chapter 19

Dawn saved and closed the document she had been editing on. She had finished making corrections on the scene where Greta had lost everything in a fire and her husband had tenderly comforted her.

She felt drained from putting so much emotion on the paper and she felt very alone.

She wanted someone to share the experience of a good writing day with.

Julie was at the doctor having an ultrasound. Denny and Xander were with her.

Her dad and Kyle had been supportive of her writing but neither had read the first book she had written. She thought about calling Wilma but then brushed the thought away. Wilma would probably be at work and she didn't want to bother her with something so inconsequential.

She stood up to stretch but the loneliness continued to plague her as she wandered around the room.

She caressed her mother's picture but even that didn't do much to alleviate her emotions. Greta had a loving husband to comfort her when Greta felt like she had lost everything. Dawn was all alone.

She almost called Isaiah but when she had picked up the phone to dial his number she froze. She had sent a text message to ask if he was feeling better and he had sent a simple *yes*. She had asked if he wanted to come over and eat the pie she had made but he said he couldn't. She hadn't heard from him since then.

She didn't know if he even wanted to talk to her. She had thought about calling or texting hundreds of times but she just hadn't been able to bring herself to do it. Besides, was it even her place to burden Isaiah with everything when he was just a friend?

She didn't know. She just knew that she was deeply lonely like she had been in the early days after she and Ben had broken up. She closed her eyes for a moment trying to collect her thoughts. She wasn't exactly missing Ben. He had lied to her and broken her heart. She wasn't even missing the memory of the love they had shared. Instead, she missed being with someone. She missed having someone to share her achievements and failures with. She had called Ben when she passed a hard test or when she had gotten a bad grade on a paper. She didn't have anyone like that in her life now. Sure, Julie supported her but Julie had her own life and that life would be even more distant once her babies arrived.

Dawn's phone beeped and she glanced down at the message. Her heart fell when she saw it was from Julie instead of Isaiah.

Two girls and a boy.

Dawn smiled at the message then she frowned. It was another piece of news she didn't have anyone to share with.

"What exactly do you do?" Frank asked looking at Isaiah's application.

"I just started an internet business. Before that I was doing handyman work. I am still looking for something steady but I have enough for a deposit and three months rent. I was hoping that would be enough," Isaiah said. He forced a smile. Four other apartment complexes had turned him down. This was the last one in town that had an apartment available at a price he could afford. The buildings were older which he assumed was why they were so cheap to rent. They had linoleum floors instead of carpeting and the gas stove in the one he viewed had seen better days. A radiator heated the apartment during the winter and he would have to install a window air conditioner for the summer.

The apartment's one bedroom was small and attached to a tiny bathroom. The living room, dining room, and kitchen were combined into one room. It was smaller than Pete's apartment but it would meet his needs. He just had to convince the property manager that he could afford the apartment. He would find a way. He had to. He needed the apartment. He needed to have some prospects, no matter how small, before he could ask Dawn to start dating him. He intended to marry her. That was one thing he had realized. If he had never had botulism and never come to Ohio he wouldn't have met the Millers or Dawn. She was a woman who could understand him. She could believe in his dreams. Like him, she was a dreamer. He needed a woman like that.

"Our property owner has very specific rules for our renters. I don't think I could get her approval on your application without a steady job," Frank said.

"Thanks anyways," Isaiah said. He reached out to shake the man's hand. Frank didn't take it but instead sat looking at him for a moment.

"Do you have a reference for anyone you have done handyman work for?"

"I have been working mostly for Denny Miller," Isaiah said.

"The disabled veteran?"

"Yeah. Do you know him?"

"A bit. He and my brother were friends as kids. Played some card game together. We heard when he came back in a wheelchair. Everyone who knew him was pretty devastated about it."

"He is doing well for himself," Isaiah said.

"I heard he got married."

"He has triplets on the way," Isaiah said.

"Triplets? Well that is something."

"Would you like his number so you can call for a reference?" Isaiah asked. He hoped that having someone that the apartment manager knew vouch for him would get him into the apartment.

"You can write it down so I can show my boss. We are hiring a part time handyman. Mostly someone to help when we have a move out. Also, the handyman we have is tired of calls at night and on weekends. He is getting older. Probably will retire in another five years. It isn't much but I would be willing to hire you on a trial basis."

"I need to tell you that I am a little slow. I had botulism a while back and still suffer the effects of it."

"Well, I am willing to give you a try. I can't imagine you being much slower than our current handyman," Frank said.

"I'll take the job," Isaiah said. If most of his calls were

129

at night and on the weekend it wouldn't take away from his online work and it would give him some extra stability. Maybe it would work out or maybe not but it was a step in the right direction.

"I'll give Denny Miller a call and then you can start tomorrow. Once you have been here a week or so I think we can get you into that apartment. I'll put a hold on it for you. I know you wanted to move in today but-"
"I'll take what I can get," Isaiah said and he meant it.

He hurried out to the Honda Civic he had bought the day before and slid into the seat. The interior of the car smelled of cigarettes and wet dog but it ran decently for having over one hundred thousand miles on it. The owner had been willing to sell it cheap just to get rid of it.

He folded his arms and said a prayer of gratitude.

Things were finally looking up.

Chapter 20

"Brother Denny Miller has been called to serve as Bishop. All those in favor indicate by the uplifted hand," the man at the podium making the announcement was one that Dawn knew by sight but not by name. She glanced over at Denny who looked contemplative. Julie, beside him and holding his hand, was all smiles. Dawn raised her hand.

Denny's parents and Julie's parents were seated together in the row before them. Julie's younger sister Stacy was with them though Gwen was not.

She had just lowered her hand when Isaiah slid in beside her.

"Can we talk after sacrament?" Isaiah whispered.

"Can't it wait?" Dawn asked. She thought she would be glad to see him but now that he was here she felt hurt that he had gone so long without any contact with her.

"Not really. I'm on call."

"On call?"

"I'll tell you all about it. I just need to talk to you as soon as possible and if my cell phone goes off," Isaiah indicated a sleek silver cell phone in a black case that was clipped to his belt buckle, "I will have to go."

"Alright," Dawn said. Isaiah leaned back into the pew beside her and she could feel the warmth radiating from his shoulder. It had been a long time since she had sat this close to a man at church. Last time had been with Ben in the singles ward.

She closed her eyes and tried to focus on the words flowing from the podium even as she tried to block out the feel of Isaiah beside her. It was easier to be angry at him.

"What did you have to say that couldn't wait?" Dawn asked. Her voice was terse and he wondered if it had been a mistake to drag her out of church. The feelings in his heart just felt so desperate. The idea was as persistent as water dripping from a tap.

He indicated the doors to the parking lot. This wasn't a conversation he wanted to have in the hallway even if that would have meant being able to hear the talks through the overhead speakers.

The day was crisp but not cold. Recent rain had cooled the air and autumn was just around the corner.

"I got an apartment and a job," he said.

"That is great," Dawn said though the look on her face wasn't nearly as enthusiastic as he had hoped.

"In a year, maybe less, I hope to be able to save up for a small house," Isaiah said. Didn't she understand how important all of this was to him? To them?

"I am really happy for you," Dawn said. She did smile at him but she didn't throw her arms around him and hug him as he had imagined. She lifted her right hand up to rub her left arm. He noticed that her skin had goose bumps. He hoped she wasn't too cold. It didn't seem that cold to him. Not even when a gentle breeze blew a strand of her hair across her cheek. He watched her tuck it behind her ear.

She was the most beautiful woman he had ever laid eyes on. It wasn't just her physical body either. He knew the beauty of her soul.

"It won't be nearly as nice as the Miller's house. I don't know that I can ever afford anything as nice as that but I do think it will be adequate."

"Why did you need to drag me out of church to tell me this?" Dawn asked. Her voice had softened and she was looking up at him cautiously.

"Because I want to marry you. Not right now. I guess you probably want to date first and do things the proper way but for me it will just be a formality. I have been praying for Heavenly Father to help me understand what he has planned for me and-"

"I can't," Dawn whispered.

"Can't? Did you start seeing someone else?" It hadn't been that long since they had talked. Certainly not enough time for her to become deeply involved with a man she had just met. She might have gone on a casual date or two but that was why he had made sure his intentions were clear. He had no interest in dating her. He wanted to marry her.

"I am not seeing anyone," Dawn said. He felt relief flow through him. She wasn't seeing anyone else. He wasn't too late.

The cell phone on his belt began to vibrate.

"I have to take this," he said. He pulled the phone from the holder and flipped it open. The tenant in 42 B had a leak in her toilet. He assured her he would be there as soon as he could.

"You need to go," Dawn said.

"I do. It is this new job. I can come by after church and-"

"No, Isaiah, you need to go," Dawn said. He could see her eyes filling with tears but they didn't fall as she turned around and went back inside.

He wanted to follow her but he knew he didn't have the time. The tenant in 42 B needed his attention and he couldn't lose the job he had. He wasn't giving up on Dawn. He just needed to take care of his work first. He took one more glance at the church doors before turning around and climbing into his car.

"I thought you might be here," Julie said putting a hand on her shoulder. After she had fled from Isaiah she had needed time alone. There was one room at church where she was almost guaranteed it. She had gone into the nursing mother's room which was rarely occupied and thrown herself down on the worn red chair in the center of the room before the tears began to fall in earnest. Once they had started she hadn't even tried to stop them. She wasn't sure how much time had passed. Relief Society might be starting or even over. Dawn had no idea.

"I am alright," Dawn whispered.

"I am sure you are but do you want to tell me what has you so upset."

"Isaiah wants to marry me," Dawn said. She felt more tears pour down her cheeks.

"And you don't want to marry him?" Julie asked.

"I do want to marry him," Dawn said. Julie handed her a tissue and she wiped her eyes and then blew her nose. It sounded like a steam engine docking.

"I don't think I understand," Julie said. She tried to sit

on the arm of the chair but her protruding belly made any kind of balance that she might have intended impossible and so instead she leaned her back against the wall. Dawn knew she should get up and forfeit her chair but she didn't have the strength within her to move. Not yet.

"I was going to marry Ben. When I met him he seemed so strong in his testimony. He had just come back from his mission and was proud to boast of the number of converts he had baptized. He could quote scripture on any topic you could imagine. We had some of the best talks about the gospel. He was this devout man who loved God and loved the church. Or he seemed to. When he wasn't with me he was out drinking and going to parties. I thought I knew who he was but I actually didn't know him at all."

"It is difficult to ever know anyone. Are you afraid that Isaiah isn't what he seems?" Julie asked. She handed Dawn another tissue as fresh tears flowed.

"Ben had a good upbringing. I met his parents. His father had been a bishop at one time. His mother was the Relief Society president. Ben had gone to seminary every day. He had served his mission. If someone like that can lose his faith what hope does someone like Isaiah have? He got so sick on his mission that he was sent home. He has trouble working because of his illness. His parents won't talk to him because of his faith. How can a man with so much against him stay faithful if someone like Ben can't? How can I marry him knowing all he has going against him? How can I risk my eternal happiness and that of my children on a man who has been through so much? What if I marry him and in another year or two he decides that he can't keep the faith any longer? Suppose we have a baby and he decides that the church isn't worth keeping his parents out of his child's life?" Dawn said. Until that moment of outpouring she hadn't really known what she was feeling but once the words started falling from her lips she could see her personal truth and she knew exactly what she was afraid of.

"Dawn, any person can lose their faith. No matter how they were raised or what they have been through. Any man you decide to marry might someday turn his back on God. Look at King David. He was such a devout servant of God but he lost his faith at one point enough to commit adultery and murder. God helped him slay a giant and put him on the throne but he still fell to temptation. There is no man who you could marry who would be immune to temptation. That doesn't mean that Isaiah will turn his back on his faith like Ben did though. He might. He also might not. Maybe Ben had never had his faith tried before. Isaiah has. Isaiah went on his mission and became severely sick but he didn't lose his faith. He lost his parents but he didn't lose his faith. Maybe the trials Isaiah has been through will allow him to withstand temptation," Julie said.

"I just don't think I can," Dawn whispered. It was all too much. Isaiah had a new job and a new life. She had just published her first book. Julie was having triplets. Isaiah had asked her to marry him. It felt as if her head was spinning.

"Why don't you pray about it," Julie said.

It was the right answer. It was the answer that was always given whenever she was struggling but she wasn't even sure what to pray except to simply ask "what do you want me to do?" There were too many uncertainties in her life and she didn't feel like she could tackle any of them.

"I want to go home," she whispered.

"Okay. I'll have Denny drive us," Julie said reaching down to stroke her hair.

It felt like she had when Ben had broken her heart. It was the same exhausted weight of heartache she was feeling now that she had felt then. She didn't think she had strength to get out of the chair but she forced herself to and she stumbled out to the car to wait for Denny and Julie.

Chapter 21

Isaiah pulled his car into the Miller's driveway. He had given Dawn more than forty-eight hours to collect herself but he didn't intend to give up on her. Even if she wasn't returning his calls.

Denny's car was absent from the driveway as was Dawn's but that didn't stop him from knocking on the front door. He listened but there was no noise from inside. He had hoped to at least catch Julie. She might know what was happening.

He picked up his cell phone and dialed Dawn's number but it went straight to voicemail.

He tried Denny's phone with the same result.

He shoved his phone into his pocket and looked around. He could wait for someone to come home but it could be hours. This was the third time he had been to the house that day.

He turned around to return to his car but behind him he heard a door open and he whirled around. For a moment he stood looking confused at the still closed door of the Miller's house. Then, he saw a flash of color from the corner of his eye.

"Hello there," a woman on the neighboring porch called to him. She was elderly. Perhaps in her seventies. She was a thin woman with gray hair.

"Hello," Isaiah said with a wave.

"Are you looking for the Millers?" She spoke slowly and her voice croaked.

"Yeah," Isaiah said with a nod.

"I don't know when they are likely to be back. They came in yesterday just for an hour or so to get a change of clothes to take the hospital."

"Hospital?"

"Yes. Poor Mrs. Miller. An ambulance came and took her away Sunday evening." The woman wrung her gnarled hands.

"Do you know where they took her?"

"Can't say that I do," the neighbor said.

"Is she going to be alright?"

"I haven't heard," she said.

"Thanks," Isaiah said. He got back into his car and leaned back against the seat. Dawn wasn't avoiding him as he had feared which he was glad of. On the other hand, Julie was his friend and he couldn't help but be worried for her and her babies. He had put up cribs for those babies. They had to be alright. He bowed his head and said a prayer.

Dawn looked up as the shadow fell over the hospital doorway.

"Isaiah," Julie said with a smile. Dawn wanted to kick herself. She hadn't even thought to call him. Things had happened so fast.

"How are you?" Isaiah asked as he slowly entered the room. He looked like he was afraid that his presence might in some way cause Julie harm.

"Better than I appear," Julie said with a laugh.

"What happened?"

"There are just some concerns about my blood pressure," Julie said.

"But they can fix it?" Isaiah asked.

"They are trying. If not they are going to try to keep me stable for as long as possible. Then, they will have to deliver the babies," Julie said. Dawn didn't add that the babies were on the cusp of viability. The doctor had said that if they were born now they might survive or they might not. Julie had seemed unconcerned by the prognosis. Dawn hadn't tried to pull her back down to reality. Anything that kept Julie's spirits lifted had to be good for her blood pressure and the babies' health.

"How did you find us?" Julie asked. She seemed pleased that Isaiah had tracked them down.

"I went to the house. A neighbor said that you were in the hospital. I called around until I found you," Isaiah said.

"I'm glad you did. Denny needs the company," Julie said. She sent a discreet wink Dawn's way.

"Where is he?"

"In the cafeteria. I told him he needed to eat. He just went to appease me," Julie said.

"Everyone is being very appeasing right now," Dawn said. Julie had given them quite a scare. She had come into the hallway and found Julie passed out on the floor. She had called 911 and an ambulance had been sent. Denny had been at his parents' house when it happened. They had all rushed to the local hospital where Julie was stabilized and then she was transferred to Columbus.

Denny's parents had stayed late into the night then gone home to rest. Denny had wanted to stay the night but

Julie insisted he go home. The room wasn't ideal to meet his special needs. He had reluctantly gone home but Dawn had promised to stay the night. Denny had been gone only until six in the morning then been back in the hospital. Dawn had left for a shower and to pack a bag for Julie but then returned.

"Do you need anything? A blessing?" Isaiah asked.

"Denny and his dad handled that last night," Julie assured him.

"Will you let me know what I can do to help?" Isaiah asked. It warmed Dawn's heart seeing such pain in his face. He genuinely cared about Julie.

"Why don't you take Dawn down to the chapel for a while and give her a break. I know she didn't sleep well," Julie said.

"After Denny returns. He wouldn't want me to leave you alone," Dawn said.

"Nonsense. See this panel of buttons?" Julie asked Isaiah. He nodded. "If I need something I can just push this nurse call button and the unit clerk will come over the speaker. I assure you, I can be alone for a few minutes. Besides, Denny won't be much longer."

Dawn didn't want to leave Julie but she did want to talk to Isaiah. She let the differing desires ping pong back and forth before finally giving in to Julie's wishes.

"The chapel is on the first floor. I was down there earlier. It is one of the only really quiet places in the hospital," Dawn said. The hospital was owned by the Catholic Church and so had a Catholic chapel but after the initial discomfort Dawn had felt about the unusual surroundings she had bowed her head and prayed. She had prayed for Julie and the babies. She had prayed for Denny. Then, to her surprise, she found she was praying for herself.

They made their way down the elevator and to the chapel in silence. Like the day before it was empty.

They passed the statue of the Virgin Mary and sat down in the back row of chairs.

"You are going to have quite a few calls from me. Probably half a dozen voicemails. I kind of acted like an idiot," Isaiah confessed.

The night she had confronted Ben about the pictures on social media had been the last time they had spoken. He had never tried to call and make things right. She had turned Isaiah down but he kept calling. She was glad that he felt strong enough about the rightness of their relationship for him to fight for them.

"I'm sorry. I just was scared," Dawn admitted taking his hand in hers.

"I promise I will find a way to provide for you. I know I am slower and weaker than most guys but I will do whatever it takes to-"

"I never doubted you could provide for us," Dawn said. She couldn't believe he had really thought that was the reason she had tuned him down.

"I don't understand. If you weren't worried about my trouble with jobs then why-"

"I was scared you were going to lose your faith and I couldn't handle that. Not again," Dawn said.

Isaiah felt her hands tighten on his as she looked pleadingly at him. He felt utterly confused.

"Why would you think that?" Isaiah asked.

"You have been through so much. Other men have gone through less than you and walked away from their faith," Dawn said.

"And other's have gone through more. You think Denny's paralysis is less than a bout of botulism?"

"No, of course not. But he had family and friends supporting him. You didn't have anyone."

"I always had Heavenly Father. I had the support of church friends. I have you," Isaiah said. It was true. He had never felt alone in his struggles. He might have been hurt and angry but he had never once felt completely abandoned by God. In his darkest hours he had leaned on his Father for strength.

"I can see that, now."

"I've never wavered in my faith. Never," Isaiah said. He might have wished for the burden to be lifted from him and he might have prayed for an easier path but he had not given up. Not ever.

"I've wavered," Dawn whispered. "When Ben left the church I almost did as well. I had been so sure we were supposed to be together. I had felt so strongly that we were going to get married. Then, when it didn't happen I wondered if I had imagined my feelings for him. I wondered if everything I had been doing was really how I felt. I was a convert. My mother didn't find the church before she died. I never understood why God hadn't sent the missionaries to us sooner. Why hadn't he given her a chance to know the truth? Why had he let us suffer believing we were losing her to cancer? Do you have any idea how much comfort it would have brought us if we had known in her last days that we would be together as an eternal family? My mother agonized over what would happen to us. I wanted to know what was going to happen to my mother but no one had the answers. If the missionaries could have just come sooner-"

"We have to have faith that God's timing is perfect. We can't understand why things happened the way they did. We can't see what might have happened if we had followed another path or if things had played out differently. Maybe your parents weren't ready to hear the gospel before your mother died. Maybe the missionaries would have shared the gospel but your parents would have rejected it."

"They wouldn't have. I know they wouldn't have," Dawn protested.

"You can't know that. You were just a child."

"And if I hadn't dated Ben-"

"Then maybe you would have married someone else. Maybe you wouldn't be here with me now just like I wouldn't be here with you if I hadn't gotten sick. I kept begging God to help me understand why he let me eat that potato salad. I never understood why he didn't warn me. Now, I think I do," Isaiah said. He reached his hand up to caress Dawn's hair before leaning forward and bringing his lips to hers.

As he felt the softness of her lips against his he felt totally at peace. He never wanted the kiss to end but after a moment she pulled away and he let her go.

"I don't think we should date," Dawn said. Isaiah felt the wind go out of his lungs much as it had when he was a boy and had fallen from a ladder while helping his father with repairs.

"You don't?"

"No. We both have been praying about this. Dating seems like we would be questioning God. He has been pretty clear with me about what I am supposed to do. Why don't we just go ahead and agree to get married once Julie has had the babies and everything settles down."

"I like that plan," Isaiah said. Then, he leaned forward and kissed her again.

Chapter 22

Wilma squealed on the phone so loudly that Dawn had to pull the phone away from her ear. Dawn had wisely chosen to tell her father first. His response had been much calmer. He had said "that's great" before handing the phone over to her step-mother.

"You haven't chosen a date yet?" Wilma asked.

"We want to wait until Julie has her babies and things settle down," Dawn said. She wished she could give them a date. She knew that the sooner they knew the easier it would be to get a flight out. Up until now living away from her family hadn't really bothered her. Now, she wished that they hadn't moved away to Colorado.

"We will be sure to come in early to help get everything ready. You let me know what you need me to do. I can send out announcements. I can make centerpieces. You just tell me what you need," Wilma said.

"I will," Dawn promised. She hadn't really thought much about any of the details. The wedding wasn't as important to her as being married to Isaiah. The important parts, the parts of the wedding that would take place in the temple, wouldn't need much preparation. It would only be the reception after that would take work to prepare. She would have been happy to skip over that entirely if she thought it wouldn't have broken Wilma's heart. Like it or not, she was the only daughter Wilma had.

Wilma handed the phone back to her father. She guessed her step-mother was already hurrying to her own cell phone to call her step-grandparents and other members of her step-family to announce the good news.

"Don't be planning anything too fancy. My budget can't handle horse drawn carriages and trained doves," her father teased.

"I promise to keep it simple."

"Will Isaiah's parents help set things up? I don't want Wilma to get too out of control and step on your mother-in-law's toes."

"We are going to send them a wedding announcement but I would be surprised if they even respond to it," Dawn said. She couldn't imagine how much it would hurt to know that your own parents wouldn't care about your wedding. She was lucky. The Millers and the Hawthornes were like her family in Ohio. Then there was her mother's family, her father's family, and her step-family. Her life was full of people who loved her while Isaiah was alone. Once they were married he would be supported by her large and loving family. He wouldn't be alone anymore.

"I know your mom would be really proud," her father said.

"I hope she is watching from Heaven," Dawn said.

"I'm sure she is," her father said. She felt a pang of longing for her mother but she pushed it down. God had a plan and that plan involved her mother returning to Him. She wouldn't dwell on it.

She and her father said goodbye before she hung up the phone and looked down at the list of calls she needed to make. The list seemed endless. She was glad it was such a happy announcement she was making.

"You are doing good work," Frank said when Isaiah walked into the office to drop off his rent check.

"Thanks," Isaiah said.

"Our property manager is looking into buying more properties. Maybe in Carroll, Canal Winchester, or Pickerington. If so, I bet he would hire you full time," Frank said.

"Thanks," Isaiah nodded.

"Do you like it here? If we get the other property maybe you could move to wherever you were working. It would save you on gas money," Frank said.

"I will have to talk to my fiancée about that," Isaiah said. Saying the word made him smile.

"I didn't know you were getting married," Frank said.

"It is a recent development. Won't happen probably for another six months. Maybe even more."

"Still, your apartment isn't much for someone starting a family," Frank said. He was right of course. The apartment would suit him and Dawn adequately but there was nowhere to grow a family either. He wasn't even ready to think about the future children they might have. It all seemed unreal. Even Dawn agreeing to marry him didn't quite seem like it could have actually happened.

"I guess we will just have to see what God provides," Isaiah said. From the way Frank shifted Isaiah knew he had made Frank uncomfortable. Apparently, trusting God wasn't the way most people lived their lives. He realized that there were many moments when he hadn't either. His despair when he had been without a job and without a place to call home had shown his lack of faith. It was something he would need to work on. God was generous even when Isaiah couldn't see the path ahead.

He had just gotten to the front door of his apartment when his cell phone rang. He glanced at the caller ID. It was Denny.

"Can you come to the hospital?" Denny asked as soon as Isaiah answered.

"Sure," Isaiah said sensing the alarm in his friend's voice.

"Julie needs a blessing. My dad is out of town and I can't get her dad at the office. Her blood pressure spiked and the doctors want to go in and take out the babies. I really want her to get a blessing before she goes into surgery."

"Of course," Isaiah said. He turned around and hurried to his car.

Chapter 23

Dawn rushed into the room. Julie looked much calmer than Dawn felt. Denny had called her with the new that the doctors were doing an emergency c-section and she rushed to the hospital as quickly as she could.

Denny was beside Julie. He glanced up at her then turned to the clock on the wall.

"Isaiah is on his way to help give me a blessing before I go in," Julie explained. Dawn nodded. She was glad that her future husband held the priesthood and would be able to give blessings to her and their children just as Denny could. Her mind went to Ben just for a moment. He had given up that blessing through disobedience. His new wife wouldn't have the blessings of a priesthood holder in the home. It made her a little sad for them both.

"What did the doctor say about the prognosis for the babies?" Dawn whispered.

"They are at twenty six weeks. I have had the injections to mature their lungs and a level four NICU is standing by," Julie said. Dawn noticed that she didn't look afraid. She wasn't sure if Julie was in shock or if she was just at a place of acceptance. The babies were a gift from God no matter how long they had them. Dawn knew that but she wasn't sure she could muster the faith not to be nearly hysterical if she were in Julie's position.

Isaiah and Gwen burst through the door at almost the same time. They were followed by a nurse.

"The doctor doesn't want to wait much longer," she

said.

"Just five minutes," Julie promised. The nurse nodded.

Xander helped Denny stand at the side of the bed. He anointed Julie's head. Isaiah gave Julie a blessing. As soon as their hands left her head Julie pushed the call button and the nurse rushed in. Within a moment several other people were in the room and Julie's bed was being wheeled off.

Dawn sighed. The only thing now to do would be to wait.

Isaiah sat down beside her and took her hand. She was glad he was there to be a comfort. Without him the present moment would have been unbearable.

Soft sobs came from Gwen so Dawn reached out her free hand and took Gwen's.

"It's going to be alright," Denny said. With the help of Xander he was again seated in his chair.

"It doesn't feel like it," Gwen cried.

"No matter what happens, it will be alright," Denny said. Dawn understood what he meant. He and Julie were sealed together for time and all eternity. Their children were born in the covenant. Even if the earth lives of their children were brief they would be a family again. She was sure it didn't make the prospect of losing the babies any easier but it did give an element of hope. She couldn't imagine how a family who wasn't sealed together could go through something like that. How could a family know they might lose their children and believe that those children either were gone or simply wouldn't be theirs anymore after this life?

She squeezed Isaiah's hand tighter. If she had loved

Ben more than she loved God, she might have left the church with him. She might have had children who weren't sealed to her. The idea made her shudder.

"I don't know what to do," Gwen whispered.

"Why don't we go down to the chapel and pray," Isaiah suggested. Dawn wasn't sure how long the surgery would take but praying seemed like the best idea anyone could have had. Praying would ease their minds as they waited.

"I can't," Gwen whispered.

"Of course you can," Isaiah said.

"No, I can't. God doesn't want to hear from me. Not after everything I have done," Gwen whispered.

"That is when God most wants to hear from us," Isaiah said.

Dawn hoped Gwen wouldn't storm out of the room again.

"He's right," Denny said quietly. "Do you remember the story of the prodigal son?"

"Not really," Gwen admitted.

"A father had just divided his estate between his sons. One of them ran off and squandered all the wealth he had. He finally hit a point so low that he returned to his father intending to be asked to be made a servant just so that he could eat. If his father had been truly fair that is probably what would have happened. Fortunately, his father loved him and rejoiced at his return," Isaiah said.

"We are never such terrible sinners that God doesn't want us back. The Savior died so that we could be forgiven of our sins. Any time you want, you can return to God. He will take you back. You are His daughter," Denny said.

"Any day you can choose to turn your life around. You won't be back where you started. You won't be able to erase your mistakes or the consequences from them but you can return to God. You can pray. You can ask for His help and His forgiveness," Isaiah said.

Gwen pulled her hand away from Dawn and stood up. She didn't quite run from the room but almost. Dawn sighed. Part of her wanted to chase after Gwen but she knew better. There was nothing she could say to Gwen that could help her. Isaiah and Denny had spoken the truth. She could take it or leave it. All Dawn could do was to sit, pray, and wait.

It seemed as if hours had ticked by though when the doctor came in to update them less than an hour had really passed. Isaiah kept Dawn's hand in his. It was nice to hold her hand. There was comfort in her touch and he hoped that she also was comforted by him. She would be a good wife. He understood why God commanded His children to marry. Life was such a struggle but having a companion made it bearable.

"Denny Miller?" The doctor was a young man who glanced at Denny and Xander uncertainly. Isaiah guessed this doctor hadn't met him before. Likely, the doctor was a resident just learning how to be a doctor. There had been plenty of those who had come to observe him when he was sick.

"Yes," Denny said.

"Your wife is out of surgery. She is in recovery and

doing fine. A nurse will be by in a few minutes to take you to her."

"And the babies?" Denny asked.

"They are stable for the moment. You can see them before we transport them to Children's Hospital," the doctor said.

After the doctor left Dawn picked up her phone. Isaiah didn't ask who she was calling. He already knew.

"Gwen isn't picking up," Dawn said.

"Maybe she can't hear it. I know that sometimes I don't hear my phone if it is busy around me," Denny said.

"We should go look for her and tell her what is going on," Dawn said.

"Why don't you go outside and make sure she didn't step out for some air. I will go to the cafeteria to look for her," Isaiah said.

Dawn nodded. He felt the exhaustion settling into his muscles as he made his way to the elevator and then down the long hospital hallway to the cafeteria but he pushed it away. There was no room for weakness today. He walked through the cafeteria. The staff were serving hamburgers and hotdogs but Gwen was not in line waiting for food. Isaiah entered the dining area where two rooms with yellow walls and red carpets held employees and families waiting on news of their loved ones. He looked in each booth and scanned each table but Gwen wasn't there.

He sent a text message to Dawn asking if she had any luck.

She isn't out here but I did walk by her car so I know she hasn't left.

Isaiah started to head back upstairs but then an idea came into his mind. It was unlikely but still worth a look. He wandered down the hallway. He kept his eyes sharply on his surroundings in case he and Gwen intersected each other. Then, he opened the door to the chapel.

If not for her red hair he might not have immediately known it was her. She was bent over and her face was buried in her hands. He guessed she had been crying. He hoped that her tears weren't ones of fear and pain but rather of reconnecting to God.

"Your sister is out of surgery," he whispered. She didn't look up at him but only nodded.

He turned to walk away but then hesitated.

"Gwen, I know my words have sounded harsh. I don't mean them to. They are coming from a place of caring. I know about God's love and God's mercy. I just want you to know it too and to know that we are all here for you," he said.

She nodded again without looking up and he took that as his cue to leave.

Outside of the chapel he sent Dawn a text message letting her know that he had found Gwen and told her what was happening. By the time they both got back up to Julie's room Denny was there as well.

"They will be bringing her up in just a few minutes," he said.

"How is she?"

"Peaceful. I showed her pictures of the babies. We had chosen names earlier and she wanted me to let the nurses know so that they could be called by their names instead of by letters. I did. After she is here and settled I am going to head over to Children's Hospital to be with them for a while. I have a feeling I will be going back and forth quite a bit over the next few days."

"Let us know how we can help," Isaiah said.

"I will," Denny promised.

"Can I see the pictures?" Dawn asked.

"Sure," Denny said pulling out his phone.

"The boy is Danny. We weighs the most. Just about two pounds. The identical twins, Kristen and Megan were smaller. Around a pound and a half each," Denny said slowly flipping through the pictures. The babies were small enough to fit in Isaiah's hand. Each baby had a diaper on but the diapers were huge on them. The babies were thin and their reddish-purple skin was wrinkled.

They in no way looked like the cute babies on television. Still, all three were alive which seemed like a small miracle to Isaiah. They looked too fragile to be living human babies each with a spirit that had just left the presence of God.

"Did you see the pictures?" Julie asked sleepily. Isaiah had gone home and Denny had gone to Children's Hospital to make sure that the babies got settled. From her own experience working in a hospital Dawn could guess that there was loads of paperwork Denny would be required to fill out.

Gwen was with them and had been instructed that when she was ready to leave she should text her mother and either Sister Hawthorne or Sister Miller would be by to sit with Julie. At the moment, both grandmothers were heading to the NICU to get glimpses of their first grandchildren.

"They are beautiful," Dawn said. The babies were beautiful. Seeing them sent a wave of emotions through her. Seeing the miracle of new life made her giddy and excited for the day when she and Isaiah would start a family of their own. Part of her worried whether she would be up to the task. Julie had a long road ahead of her. She would be there to help her as much as she could but until that moment she hadn't really realized all it meant to be a mother. It made her long for her own mother and it also made her vow to call Wilma and thank her for all the mothering she had done over the years. True, Dawn had never really thought of Wilma as her own mother but Wilma had cared for her and Kyle as well as she could. She had driven Dawn to volleyball practice and mutual. Wilma had been there every night to help with homework and make meals. It seemed to Dawn that so much of motherhood was just meeting the needs of children. Julie's whole life would soon revolve around feeding, diapering, and teaching three little babies. It was awe inspiring.

"What did the doctor say?" Gwen asked. Dawn wished she hadn't. She didn't want anything to damper the moment.

"They are strong and doing well. They will probably be in the NICU for at least three or four months. Maybe longer. It is hard to say and will depend on if complications arise. There could be delays and other issues as they grow but the doctor is optimistic and so am I,"

Julie said.

"How long will you stay here?" Gwen asked.

"The doctor expects three or four days. It will depend on what my body does. They want to get me out of here as soon as possible so I can be with them," Julie said.

Gwen leaned back in her chair. Apparently she had run out of questions.

"Do you remember the girl we used to work with who opened her own photography studio?" Dawn asked.

"Chelsea," Julie said with a nod.

"I think I should give her a call and see if she will come down and take some pictures. It will be my treat," Dawn said. Chelsea was sure to give her former coworkers a very reasonable rate for her services. Dawn was glad to have something to offer at the moment. It would be months before the babies were home and her help would be truly needed.

"That is so thoughtful," Julie said. "Make sure you schedule your engagement photos at the same time. Have you and Isaiah picked a date yet?"

"Not yet. We wanted to wait until we knew what was happening with you," Dawn said.

Julie reached out a hand to take Dawn's.

"You are a good friend. Still, you can't live your life around me. Not now. You have your own family to start."

"If we wait six months the babies will be home and things will be settled."

"I can watch the babies during the actual wedding," Gwen offered.

"And of course you can bring them to the reception,"

Dawn said.

"It will also be winter," Julie said.

"It doesn't matter," Dawn said. It didn't. Not really. Plane tickets for her family might even be cheaper if they planned their wedding for mid January.

"You are being silly. Why not pick a date in October. That will be before the holidays but still far enough out to give you time to plan," Julie said.

"I'm just worried life is going to be busy," Dawn said. She realized it was more than that. Getting engaged was new and she was just adjusting to it. Choosing a date and planning her wedding might bring back all the insecurities she had been feeling.

"Things can change so much in one day," Julie said with a yawn. Dawn guessed she was right. After all, Julie hadn't woken up that morning planning to give birth to three premature babies. The day she had discovered Ben's lies had been an ordinary day until it wasn't. She was sure that the potluck where Isaiah had eaten the tainted potato salad had been like any other as well. Certainly, the day her mother had come back from the doctor with a cancer diagnosis hadn't seemed ominous that morning over a bowl of Cheerios.

"Yes, they can," Dawn agreed.

She picked up her phone and sent a text message to Isaiah.

Can we meet for dinner tonight? I think we should decide on a wedding date.

Chapter 24

Dawn flipped through the pictures. They were all so beautiful that it was hard to choose just one to announce their engagement.

"I like this one best," Isaiah said. In the picture she was smiling up at him lovingly against a background of trees. A duck pond was just barely visible in the distance.

Chelsea had taken their photos at the local park.

"I do like that one. I was trying to choose between it and this one," Dawn said. In the second photo they were seated together on a cast iron bench and holding hands.

"That is a good one for scrap booking but I don't think it is the one to send out to everyone," Isaiah said. Dawn took another look at the photos and then nodded in agreement.

"I will tell Chelsea we need these made into the announcements. We will send them along with the save the date cards. I have my list of who to send them to. Have you made yours?" Dawn asked.

"Yes," Isaiah said.

"How many do you need?"

"Ten," Isaiah said.

"Just ten?" Dawn asked. Her list had well over one hundred people and she was going to order another fifty announcements just to be on the safe side as Wilma kept adding names to the list almost daily and Dawn was sure she had forgotten a great aunt or some other family member who she would remember at the next to last minute.

"I am going to send one to my parents. The rest I will send to a few friends and mission companions. Most won't be able to make it. Probably just Pete and his family," Isaiah said. It made her sad that so many people who loved her would be joining them and that Isaiah would likely have just Pete and his family.

"You really don't think your parents will come?" Dawn asked.

"Part of me imagines they will. I keep imagining coming into the church for the reception and seeing them sitting at a table. I imagine my mother hugging you and my father shaking my hand. I don't really expect it to happen though. That isn't the type of people they are. They didn't come see me when I was in the intensive care unit of the hospital. I was laying there wondering if I was going to live. People do die from botulism. The nurse told me how lucky I was. Almost every day I was in that bed I imagined my family coming to see me. They never did," Isaiah said.

"I'm sorry," Dawn whispered.

"Don't be. My parents don't know what they are doing. I've forgiven them for it a long time ago. I pray for them. I pray they will have a change of heart. I keep hoping that even if it doesn't happen in this life it might in the next," Isaiah said.

He made sure to keep his words casual but they hurt his throat to say. In the past several weeks he had seen the love and care that Denny and Julie had given to their children. They were constantly at the hospital with them.

Even though their babies had a whole nursing staff to care for them they went to the NICU to make sure that their babies knew they were loved and to give them all the caring that they were able. He had seen Denny and Julie coming home looking exhausted. He had even seen Julie cry on more than one occasion. She had claimed it was hormones and maybe she had been telling the truth but he suspected that the tears came from a place of love for her children.

His father and mother had once presumably loved him like that. He was the first child. He was sure that his mother had fed him at her breast and given him all the cuddles and love a baby could want. He had seen all the love she had given his siblings and so he had to believe she had loved him the same.

He remembered the look of pride in his father's eyes when he had learned a new skill. He had been his father's nearly constant companion. His father was the one who had taught him about the love of God and the sacrifice of Christ. It hurt his heart that now his parents were strangers. He couldn't imagine any scenario where he would withdraw love from his future children. Not even if they left the church and turned to a life of sin. Julie still loved her sister though Gwen had been making poor choices. Relations might be tense but it was clear that Brother and Sister Hawthorne still cared about Gwen even though her previous decisions didn't line up with their own values. They were a family. They had promised to love each other and be connected together for eternity. Certainly, Heavenly Father never stopped loving his children even when they stopped believing and trusting in him.

Dawn reached out and wrapped her arms around his shoulders.

"I'm sorry," she whispered.

"Don't be. You are all the family I need," Isaiah said.

"Hopefully not all the family you want. I was really hoping we would have a baby in a year or two," Dawn said.

"I will give you a house full of babies if that is what you want," Isaiah said and he meant it.

Chapter 25

Dawn pulled up the monthly report of book sales on her laptop. She had put out the third book in the Greta series the month before. Sales had been steady but nothing special. When she had published the first book she looked at her sales every day. Now, she just checked the list monthly.

She looked the numbers over carefully. She thought they had to be wrong. The sales were triple what they had been the month before. She did the royalties calculations in her head. She wasn't making a fortune but she was certainly making enough to pay her bills for the next three months.

She pulled out her phone and took a picture of the screen. Then, she sent the shot to Wilma, Julie, and Isaiah.

It was a small thing while she was planning a wedding but it still felt like a win.

Quit your job.

The message she got back from Isaiah was almost instantaneous.

She picked up the phone and dialed his number.

"Are you working?" Dawn asked. She didn't want to bother him if he was unclogging a toilet or fixing a leaky sink.

"On call," Isaiah said "but at the moment I am just sitting here. I was editing a video to upload."

"I got your text. Do you really mean it? Do you really think I should quit working at the hospital? This month's sales could be a fluke. There is no way to know if things will continue like this or not," Dawn said.

"It doesn't matter. Once Julie brings the babies home she will need all the help she can get. It isn't like you won't be working. I mean, didn't you just tell me last week about that new series you wanted to start writing?"

"Yes, but-"

"But my wife shouldn't have to work two jobs. Not when I can support us." Dawn closed her eyes. Isaiah was doing well at his current handyman job but she also knew he was still physically limited and slower than some other men would be. If she quit her job and then he lost his she wasn't sure he could find another easily.

"Are you really sure?" Dawn asked.

"Do you remember what I told Denny about having the faith to set up the nursery? God will work it out. He will lead us in the direction we should go. We have to trust him. We need to not be afraid," Isaiah said.

"You really think God wants me to write?"

"He put the desire to write in your heart and then let your dad find those notebooks that belonged to your mother," Isaiah said.

"Alright. I will do it then," Dawn said. "I will call work right now and put in my two week notice."

Dawn said goodbye and closed the phone. Her hands started to shake.

She took a deep breath and then knelt beside her bed to pray. It seemed too much to ask God to let her be the writer she wanted to be. Surely, there were more worthy things she could have asked for. She had prayed for guidance in college and in guidance about marrying Isaiah. She had prayed for the lives and health of Julie and her babies. She had prayed for the well being of her family. Still, she felt ridiculous asking her Father in Heaven to make her a writer. It felt silly asking him to help her make money from book sales. Yet, she prayed for that. She prayed for Isaiah to continue to have his job. She prayed that she would know what to write.

As soon as she stood up after her prayer she put a call into her boss and she knew in her heart it was exactly what she was supposed to do.

Isaiah felt his phone ring again. He had hung up with Dawn less than three minutes before. He hoped she wasn't having second thoughts about what he had said. He had always intended for her to quit work once they were married. Her current sales should carry her until that time even if she didn't sell any additional work.

He had known as he helped her with the first Greta book that writing was a talent God had given her. He wanted her to be able to explore that talent. It would have been wasteful not to.

He looked at the caller ID. It wasn't Dawn. The area code was the same one he had as a child in Missouri.

He swallowed hard before opening the phone.

"Hello?" Isaiah said.

"Is that really you?" asked the voice of a teenage girl. It shamed him that he wasn't sure which of his sisters it was.

"Yes, it is me," Isaiah said.

"No one knows I am calling. Not even Eliza," she said. That told him the caller was Emma.

"Where are you calling from?"

"A friend is letting me use her cell phone. Don't worry, she won't tell."

"I don't want you to get into trouble," Isaiah said. His eyes burned with tears at hearing the voice of his sister. It had been so long.

"I know," Emma said.

"How did you know my number?" Isaiah asked.

"It was on the engagement announcement you sent to mom," Emma said.

"She showed it to you?" Isaiah asked.

"Of course not. I intercepted the mail. I'm not doing very well in Math. I didn't want them to get my report card until I could change the F to a B," Emma said. The big brother part of him wanted to scold her both for her poor grade and for lying but he didn't dare too. If he did, she might never speak to him again.

"I've missed you," Isaiah said.

"Have you sent other letters to mom and dad or was this the first?"

"I've sent one every time I moved," Isaiah said.

"Has that been a lot?"

"Kind of," Isaiah admitted.

"When we asked about you mom and dad said they didn't know where you were. They told everyone that you ran away and that they hadn't been able to find you," Emma said. Isaiah could understand the lie. It wasn't even a total lie. He had left their faith which to them was probably very similar to running away.

"It wasn't quite like that," Isaiah said.

"After I saw your letter I guessed that," Emma said.

"How is everyone?" Isaiah asked. Anything she could tell him about home and their family would be a blessing.

"Eliza is better at Math than me but not half so good in English. I am taking French this year and she is taking Latin. I told her that was a stupid thing to do. I mean who goes around speaking Latin these days?"

"And Toby?" Isaiah asked.

"He isn't much of a student. They had to hold him back last year. Mom was upset but dad didn't care. He takes Toby everywhere with him. I guess he figures that if Toby isn't much good with his school books he will at least have some skills," Emma said.

"Dad is right about that. He did the same with me and I am working as a handyman for an apartment complex," Isaiah said. He didn't want to tell her about the online videos. She might have been smart enough to call him from a friend's cell phone but if she tried to look him up online she would almost surely get caught and it was hard to guess the wrath of their parents.

"I don't suppose you can come and visit," Emma whispered.

"No, I don't suppose I can," Isaiah said.

"Mom and dad kicked you out?" Emma asked.

"Yeah," Isaiah admitted.

"What did you do?"

"It is a long story," Isaiah said. Anything he said might hurt his parents and that wasn't his intention. His parents had done what they believed was right. They believed that the Mormon faith was wrong and they hadn't wanted their other children swayed to join another faith. He had seen Mormon families shun members who had left the church. He guessed that families hoped that their lost children would miss the family enough to give up their sinful ways. He doubted that strategy worked very often.

"Can I come see you?" Emma asked.

"Mom and dad wouldn't like that," Isaiah said.

"Maybe once I am older?" Emma asked.

"Of course. You are always welcomed at my house," Isaiah said and added "So are Eliza and Toby if they ever want to come."

"I hoped you would say that. Try not to have any babies until I am old enough to visit, okay? I would be so sad if I was an aunt and couldn't see my nieces and nephews."

"We will try," Isaiah said.

"Your wife is really pretty. Is she nice?" Emma asked.

"I think so," Isaiah said.

"Do you think she will like me?" Emma asked.

"I think she will love you. She has a brother but no sisters," Isaiah said.

"I can't wait to meet her," Emma said. It made Isaiah's heart ache.

"You can call whenever you like. Just don't get yourself in trouble," Isaiah said.

"Weren't you sneaky as a teenager?" Emma asked with a laugh.

"A little," Isaiah admitted.

"Then don't worry about it," Emma said. "But I need to go now. Michelle needs to use her phone. We are at the mall and her mom wants her to call and check in every hour," Emma said.

"I love you," Isaiah said. He wished he could hug his sister. Both his sisters had driven him crazy at times but he would do anything to have that craziness back now.

"I love you too," Emma said. The line went dead and Isaiah closed his phone and sighed. He hoped Emma would call again but he knew she might not find a way to do it without getting into trouble. Either way, hearing from her had been a blessing. He sometimes forgot what it felt like to be part of a family. Now, he was going to start his own and he wanted to bring into his new family the experience he had gained from the family he had grown up in. His parents had loved him and raised him to serve others and genuinely love God. He wanted to make sure he continued that tradition in his own home. Unlike the love of his parents his love would be unconditional just as God's was.

Epilogue:

Dawn held Isaiah's hand as they exited the Columbus Ohio temple as man and wife. There was a chilly breeze and the leaves around them were colored and starting to crinkle as the weather changed.

Denny and Julie were right behind them.

The Miller's and the Hawthorne's had already left as had her parents. They had gone to the church to set up the reception. Denny was driving them all to the church. Dawn had ridden to Columbus with her parents and Isaiah had been driven by Denny and Julie. Now, Denny would drive them all back to Lancaster.

"I'm glad you did this before we brought the babies home," Julie whispered. Dawn had been up to the NICU with her the day before. The babies were growing and would be ready to go home soon. Already, they required lots of care and Dawn was glad she would be able to focus on helping Julie instead of on planning a wedding.

"I'm glad we got everything moved earlier this week. I think there is rain forecasted tomorrow," Isaiah said. He had been made the primary handyman for an apartment complex in Carroll and they had moved most of Dawn's things in the day before. It would put them in a different ward though she knew she would often join Denny and Julie at church to help with the babies. Still, she had been intertwined in their lives so long that moving on to her own life felt almost like leaving home all over again.

"I am just glad it didn't rain today," Dawn said. God had given them a picture perfect wedding day which was something she was grateful for.

"Did you finish writing the holiday book you were telling me about?" Julie asked.

"Yes. I will be putting it out next month. Just as soon as Isaiah approves it," she said giving his arm a playful squeeze. She had written a holiday themed book for the Greta series. She hadn't told Julie but it was the last Greta book she planned. She wanted to start something new. She wanted to write a book that was all hers.

"Planning a wedding and moving has kept me busy," Isaiah laughed.

"I suppose we will let that excuse slide," Dawn teased. She felt giddy with joy. She was finally married to a man who she trusted and who put his trust in God. She was about to start on a new chapter of her life.

Isaiah's phone began to ring. She wished he would leave it be but he checked the caller ID and then lifted it to his ear.

"It's for you," Isaiah said after a moment of hesitation.

Dawn took the phone from him curiously.

"Dawn?"

"Yes."

"Hello. This is Emma, your new sister-in-law. I've wanted to talk to you but my silly brother was never around you when I called. Guess that won't be a problem now though."

"No, I guess it won't," Dawn said. She was surprised by how delighted she felt at talking to her sister-in-law. Isaiah had mentioned that his little sister had called him from time to time but having a voice to put to her name was refreshing.

"I sent a wedding present. It isn't much. I had to do chores for weeks to save up for it. I told my parents I was saving up for a new dress. I found a dress at the thrift store that was almost new and used the rest on your gift," Emma said with obvious pride in her voice.

"That is very kind of you," Dawn said.

"Hope you are a half decent cook. My mom is but Eliza and me aren't," Emma said. Dawn supposed the gift must be some kitchen gadget. Whatever it was, she would make sure to use it with love.

"I can cook a mean pizza," Dawn said with a laugh.

"I have to go now but I just wanted to say congratulations," Emma said.

"Thanks," Dawn said before the line went dead.

"I have a feeling that as soon as she turns eighteen we will be seeing a lot of her," Isaiah said taking back his phone.

"You can never have too much family," Dawn said. She closed her eyes for a moment and thought of her mother. She hoped her mother was watching her and proud of the woman she had become. In a few moments she would join her father, Kyle, and Wilma to celebrate the addition of Isaiah into their family. She couldn't help but think about family as they drove to her wedding reception. She had never truly understood sealings before today. Now, she understood. As a child she had been sealed to her father, Wilma, Kyle, and her mother in a chain that would one day link them all the way back to Adam in one huge family of everyone who had ever lived on earth. Now, she was linked to Isaiah and all the children that they would someday have and all the posterity after until the end of time.

"I sure am hungry. I can't wait to eat," Isaiah said.

"I remembered to tell everyone that they could bring any food they liked except for potato salad," Julie said. They all laughed.

Dawn couldn't help but think that without a mishap with a potato salad many years ago she wouldn't be in the car at that moment sharing all the love that surrounded her. Though parts of the journey had been difficult the journey had been one of joy.

God was good.

About the Author

Emma lives in Ohio with her twin daughters. She currently works at the local hospital as a Switchboard Operator.

Acknowledgments:

I would like to thank Christina for her input on this story. She is my most loyal beta reader and best friend. We met at Young Women's camp when we were 13 and have been best friends ever since.

I would also like to thank Ameshin for his beautiful cover art. You can view his gallery on deviant art.

Author's Note:

I am really enjoying writing the Happy Eternally After Series. These stories have been on my mind for years and I started the first draft to Road of Faith in 2008 while my husband was deployed to Afghanistan.

I had not initially intended to write about Dawn. She had been created as a character to interact with Julie and I had not really thought much about her initially. Then, she decided that she wanted her own story and I decided to oblige. There was an outbreak of botulism in Lancaster Ohio from incorrectly prepared potato salad. I was already employed at the hospital during the outbreak and as we were educated on botulism I realized that it would be an interesting reason to send a missionary home. The real life botulism outbreak happened at a church potluck of another denomination.

I have rough drafts for the next two books in this series but one of my beta readers recently suggested another two books I could add on. I am sure that this series will be at least four books long but it is quite possible it could end up even longer than that. I hope you will continue on this journey with me.

If you would like to e-mail me you can do so through my publisher. Their e-mail is BZPublishingllc@gmail.com

Thanks so much for reading.